THE SEARCHES

THE SEARCHES

Finding Plane and Mystery

R.Evans Pansing

Order this book online at www.trafford.com
or email orders@trafford.com

Most Trafford titles are also available at major online book retailers.

Printed in the United States of America.

ISBN: 978-1-4669-0448-4 (sc)
ISBN: 978-1-4669-0449-1 (e)

Library of Congress Control Number: 2011960884

Trafford rev. 05/07/2012

 www.trafford.com

North America & international
toll-free: 1 888 232 4444 (USA & Canada)
phone: 250 383 6864 ✦ fax: 812 355 4082

Cast:

Dickson Straight—Young man of many talents
Luther (Lunch Box) Locke—Boyhood friend of Dickson
Sprig Gardner Beautiful young lass with charm and
    tenacity
Herb Gardner—Missionary and father of Sprig
Bump—Sprig's mule
Monty—young native boy
Randall—Herb's helper

PROLOGUE

S OME TIME AGO when electronic gadgets were not yet in evidence, the need for on-foot investigations of lost items were the norm. In the great jungles of the African continent were just beginning to open up to progress and civilization the need for explorers and adventurers was deemed necessary. Dickson Straight and Luther Locke were young men (or boys) that were on the look out for things to do when a call came to them to search and locate a downed plane that had medical supplies and a mine payroll. The pilot of the plane was a distant relative of Luther (Lunch box.) Locke causing the young man to easily volunteer for the search and rescue. Dickson Straight, Luther's closest friend was already in the area when the call came to prepare and wait for Luther to begin the search. Dickson liked adventure and waited for his friend with anticipation and adequate supplies. Both young men would eventually know this hunt to be more important than just one search. Decisions or events in youth oft—times have lifetime consequences.

CHAPTER ONE

THE GOING WAS difficult but rewarding even though I was thinking of giving up. The results could be devastating if not properly executed. I had run from evil. I had flown from evil. I had even climbed away from evil. This fear and trepidation on my part was enough to force me into a swimming mode to avoid a dangerous confrontation. I jumped into the cold and foreboding river as black as ink and began my breast stokes in earnest as the race was on, I thought. Evidently, they could not swim, as well as the fact that the river was a torrent at flood stage. Shaking their fists and kicking the water's edge they seemed to be frustrated as well as bewildered at my narrow escape from them only to thrust myself in the arms of a raging, deadly river.

It all began at the jungle bar where I was waiting for my friend and partner Luther Locke. Luther was a big man and a colleague of mine for several years. We had befriended each other in our days back in the States. He was of a friendly nature with a high intelligent forehead and green eyes that were of a piercing nature. Reddish hair topped his infectious smile. We had been on several adventures together. His name was Luther Locke and mine is Dickson Straight. I am a guide in the wild jungles of this forgotten land. I am of medium build and brown hair and blue eyes that had seen a lot of life in my 24 years. A college grad but still with some wanderlust in my veins I had taken on the guide job as a kind of lark. Little did I know when I accepted this job it would take me on a journey that changed my life forever. My first encounter with future complications was at a small outpost bar in the jungles interior. There I waited for Luther Lunch Box Locke to join me when my attention was drawn to a local person. The old man just sort of melted into my presence so that to ignore him would be to offend him. This old withered man took up my time at the bar. He was trying to sell me a treasure map. It was old and inscribed on a lambskin of an ancient age. I knew that the effort on my part was foolish. When would I ever buy a treasure map from a shriveled up old, seedy, dirty beady eyed vagrant? I was just burning time when I noticed that the forearm of the wizened salesman of the map had a tattoo. It was quite faded with age but on close examination, I became aware that the marks on his arm were coinciding with the scrawlings on the map. I bought the map. It would be a good conversational piece if nothing else. The ink was faint but if held up to some bright light I was certain the lambskin would reveal details not seen here in the darkened jungle bar.

I finally left the bar with my heavy backpack and wandered around trying to locate a safe and secure place to bed down for the night. Luther Locke would have no trouble locating me, even in the night. His talent for tracking was without equal.

Locating a likely spot, I turned around to see three evil-looking men following me. They had been in the bar and listened with ears and eyes that spelled trouble, if ever I did see any. I took my backpack off and carefully concealed it in some heavy brush when I was out of their line of sight. Back on the trail I was again in their sight so I began to walk rapidly towards the river hoping some boatmen would be available for a degree of safety.

Reaching the river, I was disappointed that no one was around. I was certain that the three malcontents were closing in for the kill or robbery. There was no welcome or helpfulness in their body language. My only course of action at this point was to out-swim them. I had been a first class swimmer in college so without any heavy thinking I entered the water with an icy splash. It was only seconds before I realized that my rash action was one of dire consequences. The river was at flood stage here in the land of surprises. Making my way in the water, swimming for the far bank I was assailed with floating brush and debris of all kinds. Nearing the opposite bank, I was hit on the head by a heavy object that turned me upside down as the stars gathered for a light show. Not knowing up from down I completely relaxed for a second to allow my body the luxury of finding the surface. When my head eventually bobbed to the surface, I saw the bank close at hand. Grasping out for some safety I found only roots and slippery mud for my landing. Using all my strength, I purchased a foothold and landed on the bank with some gasping that indicted to me how close I had become to a floating stiff on this raging river. The thought grabbed my heart when I realized I must somehow swim back for there was for my pack. I knew there was no bridge or crossing for miles. Lying there, I looked up at the sky to see only a black void. Where have the stars gone? Closing my eyes, sleep overtook me and sent me off to a place of indescribable tranquility.Sounds of a threatening nature aroused me from my exhausting slumber or was it a stupor?

Raising my head to half-mast I painfully squinted towards a few warthogs in the vicinity of my near demise. It would soon be morning, according to my mental calculations formed from the faint gray in the sky. I must be downwind from the grunts and guttural sounds from the happy swine. They didn't bother me but they looked ferocious so I was encouraged to get up, shake off my pain, and begin to plan a way and time to re-cross that body of water. Feeling my scalp, I was surprised to find a lot of clotted blood and a lump the size of a hurting egg at the place a submerged log must have given me an unwelcome smack.

I looked across the river and was glad that no native was waiting on the other side for me to return. Going back down to the river's edge, I spent a lot of time gathering the courage to again cross that watery obstacle. Looking at the rush of the brown liquid, I had flashbacks of the nighttime swim that caused my head to ache and swell. My clothes were still wet so I decided I might as well begin to walk up stream before entering the watery torrent. I must travel about the same distance above from the jungle bar as I had been pushed downstream last night. About a quarter of a mile of traveling, upriver I spied the place I had entered the river. No one was on the bank there either. I felt that the three thieves had assumed me drowned by the aqueous barrier or by the beasties of the jungle. I continued up river about the same distance and found the river here much wider, meaning a longer but less rigorous swim. Entering the water was the more difficult part of the swim because of my confidence was wavering. The water was not as cold but very threatening. Engaging my breaststroke, I made good time across the waters of the flooded river. Reaching the opposite bank, I had a much easier time exiting onto a sandy area that was flat but occupied with several startled crocodiles. They moved off as I moved up to the primitive road and began a careful return to the jungle bar. I was to meet my friend Luther Locke there to begin a search for his uncle who had reportedly crashed his small plane with medical supplies requested by one of the missionary outposts. With the stealth of a chameleon I crept back to the low squat building to determine if it would be safe to enter, The bar was vacant of all human inhabitants, only flies seemed to habitat the empty building. Only on closer inspection did I notice a dog of giant proportions guarding the beer and spirits. This was an encouragement to return to my concealed backpack and do my waiting some small distance from the bar. The backpack was undisturbed and waiting for me at its concealed location. I set up camp down the road that led to the bar and began my waiting. I observed only a few natives passing on the road from my concealed position, going about their chores for the day. My waiting was rewarding about midday after a nap and few pulls on my beef jerky. Luther Locke came ambling down the road with his pack, chewing on something. His nickname was Lunch Box because he always seemed to have food somewhere on his person. It might be a sandwich or crackers; maybe even an apple or two. Exiting from my hiding spot Luther noticed me where upon he gave out a boisterous greeting. "There you are! My old friend Dickson Straight waiting for me just as promised. You look like last week's lumpy pudding"

"What took you so long? I have been here two days just out of death's grasp by hanging around the jungle bar you suggested we meet."

"Hold on old friend. I had to find some nourishment to keep me in shape for this trek into the jungle. What is that egg size knot on your head? How have you escaped tragedy so early in our quest?"

I explained the night's happenings to Lunch Box as we began to move into the un-chartered jungle. He wanted to stop in the bar for a little refreshment but I convinced him to begin our search without the bar's little unexpected surprises. With only a "shucks," to measure his displeasure we both set off to find the plane and medicine. We entered the thick vegetative growth on what might be called a faint animal trail. The day was getting hotter as the sun progressed towards its zenith in the sky. All kinds of bugs and flying insects were busy notifying their kin of our location as well as our tender succulent flesh. The limbs and branches of tree and shrubs alike gave their customary slaps and whacks until we were ready to quit for a rest on a little hill that gave us a view of the surrounding terrain. This location also provided us with some shade of the kind that was not seen too often on these little hillocks. Looking at our back trail, we thought we caught a glimpse of movement, revealed by the movement of brush and limbs in the distance. Luther gestured that his revolver was at the ready for any trouble making actions. We decided to just wait and see what was following our progress. While we waited, Lunch Box provided us with some hand held vittles. A short time later, some people were sighted coming up the hill carrying produce on their heads in a very peaceful manner. They looked straight ahead, as they passed, not noticing us as threats or hostile. We smiled, but received little or no recognition as the little group passed us verifying the trail we were on was leading us in the right direction and not a croc or lion trail. Pulling burrs from each other's clothing, we spent an enjoyable few minutes of rest and relief. I was hesitant to pull out the treasure map and show it to Luther.

Old Lunch Box was noted for his enthusiasm for adventure, throwing all caution to the wind and bulldogging forward with only some food in his pockets. I thought it best to keep moving forward to the plane's location with its medical supplies. I had forgotten to tell Luther about the mine's payroll also on board the downed plane. That information could also be kept from Lunch Box to be divulged later.

The planes location was sent to his base, the place in the city where the pilot had plotted his trip. Trying to keep the flight's purpose there had been little chatter on the waves to the pilot's home base. I found out the catastrophe because I had been at the base when the distress call went out. Since it was determined, I had planned to trek in that area as well as the fact the pilot was a kin of Luther. The head of the base decided that I would be the one to try and find Luther's uncle (once or twice removed),Scatter Moore. It was a task I accepted with approval because I would need something like this to keep my friend and colleague, Luther Locke, interested and intrigued with our jungle trek. Receiving the plane's last known location I was prepared to ask Luther to go with me. After all, it was his Uncle Scat Moore we were trying to locate and help. Spending days or weeks in a hot and buggy jungle looking for exotic plants for the medical community's experimentation for new drugs was not Luther's cup of tea. Only I had an appreciation of that endeavor. He had decided to accompany me because of our close friendship and his need to shed a few pounds in a hostile and controlled environment.Looking up from my musings I was surprised to see Luther calling for a continuation of our advancement down the hill and on to the plane's last known site. He so wanted to help the missionary's to receive the needed medical supplies that his sense of danger was put aside. Uncle Scat was not his favorite Uncle but family still.

I knew that the jungle was fraught with dangers of all kinds, including the human one's that might know about the miners payroll. I was carrying my trusty thirty-eight and a hunting knife, both concealed in my cargo vest. Knowing Lunch Box, he had brought some kind of weapon. The three culprits that had pursued me for evil might have known about the payroll or just wanted information that they could use for their own immoral gain, or maybe the treasure map.

Following Luther down the hill and into the bush I was reminded how blessed I was to have him as a friend and confidant. Lunch Box was not fat but considered hefty without any excess fat to be found. He did like to eat but he also was moving all the time to burn up any lurking fats or carbohydrates. He was knowledgeable in all the biologically arts with some martial arts thrown in for good measure. Luther was much smarter than he let on or appeared. One Lunch Box Locke aced all of his courses at the university we both attended. Any jokes about his rotund body or his eating habits were soon put to rest after a face-to-face meeting with his tormentors. The subject then never came up again by anyone even remotely acquainted with Luther. Only his closest friends uttered his nickname, Lunch Box, in his presence and only then with awe and reverence. Our friendship was mutually rewarding. As a team, we were Beef and Brains on one end, charisma, and audacity on the other end. The fact that I was designated leader long ago in our adventures cemented these truths.

We were now moving through the bush with a certain fluidity that indicated a well-used trail. Would we be so fortunate when arriving closer to our destination or would we have to hack our way through uncharted, injurious under—growth of the most detrimental kind? Only time will tell thought I, as an opening of some size appeared up ahead. Luther held up his hand for a time of stealth and contemplation. Coming close, he whispered in my ear.

"This clearing is too ripe for not being full of huts and barking dogs."

"How close can we approach without being discovered," I said with a tight hoarseness in my throat."Luther answered with tenseness in his voice. "It won't make much difference because all I can see are charred remains of huts in a circle. Come closer and you can see the utter destruction for what had been a native village, sometime ago. If you come closer, you will see human bones scattered around in a deadly array of finality."

I saw them white and bleached in the summer sun."This must have happened a while ago. The hyenas and jackals have made a real clean up with ants and bugs finalizing the repulsive scene. Its like the cemetery blew up on Halloween night." I was shocked by the apparent carnage that didn't seem to faze Luther as much. Luther was already with some suppositions as to the explanation of the repulsive scene.

"This was probably the result of tribal cleansing. The neighboring tribes when confronted with disease of sinister or mysterious nature come to the affected village and cleanse it by fire and by a wave of the death angel's wand. It could also be the result of slave traders coming to a village and taking only the strong and saleable people. The rest are then dispatched to the arms of the angelic host." Some of Luther's resident Christianity popped up occasionally."Well what ever it was, I suggest we leave this place and keep on track for the plane's possible location. Slave traders would love plane parts and payroll monies regardless of the pilot's condition."

"Good advice old bean. We will just stay on the perimeter of the clearing to avoid disturbing any tribal traditions."

Luther was in rare form as he moved carefully around the clearing with calculated movements. On or about the other side we entered the trail that continued farther into the bush. The area was now thick with vines and branches crowding into the once clear path, now apparently unused. We both wondered what had happened to the few people that had passed us much earlier. We decided these folks could just disappear into the bush, unseen, and unheard. We also hoped we could do the same. The day wore on to the point that evening came upon us suddenly because we were now entering a depression that ended by a rock wall at least two hundred feet tall. This would be an ideal place to make camp as it afforded us safety on at least one or two sides. We found a clearing not far from a silvery waterfall that would provide us with water.Removing the packs was difficult because of its position on backs for so long. We hadn't even removed them when we had some food at a midday break. We felt it was more important to keep moving. The packs contained everything we needed. A tent, sleeping bag, mini stove, staple food, and utensils. As Lunch Box made a fire, I set up our tent. When I had finished, I moved to the fire where Luther was already putting on coffee water.The area looked so peaceful and serene with the little dancing waterfall complete with the sounds and smells of a verdant Eden. How were we to know danger lurked all about us? Poisonous snakes were one danger plus animals of the meat eating variety. We also had many species of vegetation in the vicinity that would kill or wound the unwary. When we had finished cooking and eating supper we sat about the campfire enjoying the fresh brewed coffee when an arrow split the air and smacked close by my head.

"Dickson are you all right," blurted my friend as we both hit the ground. I pulled out my thirty-eight and fired into the bush where I had thought the arrow must have been shot. Hearing no sounds of distress we stayed close to the ground exchanging plans and possibilities. Luther had also taken a shot with his trusty Luger. We hugged the earth for about ten minutes behind some boulders. When no other signs of aggression were experienced, we rose up from our prone position to find no one in the immediate vicinity. "Well if that doesn't take the cake to destroy our peace and tranquility, I don't know what would," I said with clenched teeth and a wary look all about. "We will have to have a sharp lookout all night just to be safe. Probably four hours on and four hours off."

Luther was in perfect agreement as we finished our coffee and began to clean up the campsite, always with one eye scanning the perimeter of our clearing. He was also in agreement that we would scale the wall to avoid the long and tedious hike around this great wall of stone. Our packs contained all the necessary climbing gear, such as pitons, bongs, and carabineers. We knew it was dangerous doings but essential to save time. We took turns standing guard through the night. Each one of us got some quality sleep during our down time so that when the sun began its daytime mode we were rested and eager to get going up the wall. A breakfast light but energizing was a Lunch Box extravagance. Dried fruit puffed up by water as well as some canned meat fried to a golden brown. Rolls and jam were offered as an unexpected treat. This having been completed we finalized our morning repast with hot steaming mugs of thick cocoa for the extra energy we would soon need.

Getting out my climbing gear, Luther came over to me with the arrow that had been shot at us yesterday. "Look old bean. This arrow appears to made by a native with little skills or of a hasty nature. The shaft is barely straight. The point is a very small sharp stone and the shaft's end has what looks like fur instead of feathers." That arrow does look like a very immature creator crafted it. Maybe it was some one we should fear less since it did not find its mark? It may have been your disgruntled threesome," said Luther with some sarcasm in his voice. "Its a wonder that they missed you for these jungle people need to be expert in bow and arrow if they want to eat."

"I always fear projectiles aimed at me because the target is so ample and abundant. No harm done and no strange sounds or movements during the nighttime. Let's just saddle up and climb up this wall without any trepidation. We can be on top before lunch even though I might need to hang awhile when half way up for a light treat." Luther was on a positive roll. "Come on Dix. You go up first as always and keep me safe with that safety line and with well placed pitons."

It took a few minutes to pack up tight with heavy packs and glances all around for possible interruptions. I would go first with handholds and place pitons or bongs in any likely place to secure a safety line for Luther to follow with a degree of confidence. The first few feet always seemed the hardest even though only several feet off the flat ground. The stone was hard and conducive to climbing with some crystals and ridges. The pack's weight would get heavier as we progressed up the wall but it seemed to be as though a bungee cord was pulling at me now with only a few feet gained. The sweat began to run down my face with a blinding bight on my eyes. It was hard to focus so I was left with feeling the surface for any desirable holds. Standing on a tiny ledge, I was able to wipe my eyes clean of the burning perspiration. On belay, I shouted to give Luther the signal to CLIMB. Holding the safety line, I looked down to see his tousled reddish hair moving up the cliff's face. This sequence was repeated all through the morning with only a short rest midway, to feed our exertions and refresh our bodies with food and water. The climb was not as difficult as first thought. The wall gave many possibilities for holds. Only the weight of the packs made the going arduous. By early afternoon, we had reached what had appeared to be the top. To our mild amazement, the top ledge we had purchased was only the first step in a continuing knob. The ledge or out cropping gave way to circumvent the higher region. This would have to be a path to the plateau behind this great hump of rock. Pulling all our climbing gear and repacking we headed out to go around this hindrance in our trek to the downed plane. On one side of Mt. Hindrance, we found a small copse and with exhausted bodies made camp. Not much more than a thicket, the campsite gave us some protection from prying eyes and blustery winds at this elevation. Prying off each other's pack from our sweaty, weary persons we just collapsed on terra firma for a much needed rest. This camp was more relaxed as we were certain that no one was in the area of this wind swept ledge. We also knew that anything was possible when on a mission that included medical supplies and a substantial payroll. The three brigands below would take a full day to circle the mountain and gain the plateau.

Luther was busy with the foodstuffs so I made my self-useful by setting up the tent and making the usual necessities for a comfortable camp. Luther's fire was small because of the scarcity of fuel on this ledge on the backside of this mountain. He had constructed a stone ring to conserve the heat. The smoke was minimal and was dissipated quickly by the breezes.

With my glass, I made sweeping observations of everything in the distance hoping to spot the plane or its wreckage. No black or charred spots were to be seen. I did spot a place that would be possible for a village clearing to sustain a small group of natives. In the far distance, I saw what might be the buildings of the mine. I made notes of the findings to facilitate our trek to the most possible area of the plane's wreckage. I returned to the fire and Luther's sumptuous repast.

Beans, stew, all served with his famous fry pan bread was the fare for the evening meal. Dried figs completed our meal to our satisfaction. Lunch Box's hot coffee made with the care of a Parisian chef was the final joy of the evening's gastronomical endeavors. We just lazed about for a time enjoying the fruit of our labors at this scenic spot.

Looking down the path that we would take the next morning we were stunned to see something coming up the trail towards our campsite. A horse and rider were advancing up the narrow rock at an uncommon pace. It was not our imaginations running away with us at this altitude. Luther's exclamation was one of surprise and disbelief. "Hey Dix! Am I seeing things or is that a horse coming up the trail with a rider in a hurry?

"You're not seeing things Lunch Box. But I think I am seeing things. The rider appears to be of the female persuasion. Also an unheard situation in this part of the world."

Even more fantastic was the fact the rider was not on a horse but on a mule. The rider and mule made the last hundred yards in a more subdued pace, as the trail was steeper.

The rider was a young lady in here early twenties. No doubt a beauty in any land or on any horse or mule. She has a high intelligent forehead, intense flaxen hair, and lips full and as inviting as a pure natural red raised rose petal. Her skin was without blemish but had the hue of tan that indicted a robust outside girl. She is the owner of a turned up nose and tight chin with eyes of azure sky blue. Her form was slender but very shapely and healthy. I thought this could be the very girl I will marry some day.

Sliding off the mule she came to us out of breath and in a state of anxiousness that gave me a fright. She stood stock still in front of us and addressed us as long lost friends.

"You were sent to us by our people in the city to bring medical supplies?"

It was more of a question that a statement.

"Yes. We are trying to get down to the plateau after we have eaten and rested. Actually, the supplies you mention were to be sent by a small airplane that has been reported down in the jungle. How did you get that mule?

"The miners who are on the rampage now because they have not received their pay for the last month gave it to us a while back before the uprisings. The miners are beginning to filter back into the jungle with revenge on their minds directed to anyone they happen to meet. That is what I have come to warn the bearers of medical supplies. I assume that is you? We have been looking for you for a few days hoping you would get through without any mishaps. What about the downed plane? We hadn't heard at the mission. Our radio is not working."

I was mesmerized by her intensity but I replied." The plane is down and we are to search for It. What is your name?"

"My name is Sprig Gardner. My father is Herb Gardner, the missionary at the Masi Mission in lower Tanika."

"We are exhausted by our climb so we feel we must stay the night on the mountain and begin again in the morning to descend to the plateau."

Luther approached with his mile wide grin after listening to the conversation with Sprig.

"You must stay here since it is so late in the day. You can sleep in the tent and Dix and I, Luther Locke, will gladly sleep under the stars in our very warm sleeping blankets. You can keep cozy warm with your clothes on and our meager blanket."

Sprig was a little dubious but soon acquiesced after smelling some of Lunch Box's cooking. Sitting around the fire and eating Luther's culinary offerings, Sprig was a fountain of information about the surrounding areas and the dangers that were growing by the hour because of the miner's uprising.

"The jungle is full of terror the likes of which we have not seen for several years. Do you have any medical supplies with you?"

Luther's continence fell like an autumn leaf, slow but sure."We are on a search mission to find the lost airplane that was bringing you supplies and the miner's payroll. By all accounts, the small plane had to crash land somewhere in the interior before he could land at the mission's landing field. We have only a sketchy idea where the plane is located by the pilot's last transmission."

Sprig watched Luther with a schoolgirl's riveted attention. You could see she was full of questions but chose to stifle them for now.

The sky was beginning to fade as longitudinal clouds of blue berry hue became topped with peach light so that the scene was ethereal. Sprig looked at the sky for some time while I looked at Sprig. It was a time of remembrance for the ages

I was all for turning in to get a good nights sleep before our difficult trip down towards the plateau. The night was falling fast as we prepared to get some sleep. Sprig was content to wrap in a blanket in the tent with all of her clothes on and a pack for a pillow. Luther found a protected spot near the mountain wall and I settled down in between two boulders. My mind wandered over the last several days' events. A hurried call to begin a search. Contacting Luther Locke to accompany me as soon as possible Selecting a place to meet in the jungle. Determining an approximate time. Waiting for Lunch Box at the jungle bar. An old man eking out his final days, trying to sell me a treasure map of dubious authenticity. Three crooks trying to rob or kill me for an unknown reason. Having an arrow shot at us for no reason. Sprig the daughter of the missionary arriving with news of native uprising in the area we think the plane went down. A real quandary and I hadn't even told Luther about the treasure map yet. With all of these thoughts rattling around my head, sleep finally overtook me.

CHAPTER TWO

W E BEGAN TO break camp and load all of our supplies onto the mule whose name was Bump for obvious reasons. With this task completed, we persuaded Sprig to climb aboard, as Luther and I would walk beside her and the mule. Old Bump made his way slowly down the trail with a certain expertise most horses would not possess. The stones under the mule were slippery. Luther, and I found the going difficult even holding onto the mule and his trappings. The trail was very narrow with steep rock on one side and empty space on the other side.

The mountain was not of usual volcanic origin but was a line of hard rock ridges that ran for about 5 miles. It was a jagged outcropping of stone that one could easily call it the Devil's Backbone. We had climbed it not knowing how long the ridge ran. The three malevolent thieves no doubt knew about this and probably just made a trek around the end following paths up to the plateau. Luther was aware of this and had his gun at the ready as I also did. We did not tell Sprig of the possibility of having a run-in with these fellows.

The day had started out cool and clear but as we approached the area of lower elevation and jungle plants the air became heavy and was turning warm. The trail was now wider and more pronounced. "Too many people on this trail," I murmured. Our likelihood of proceeding without discovery was now very slim. Luther was not very talkative, even though Sprig would make copious comments from time to time to no one in particular. Her commentary was about the area and some of the hidden dangers her father had made her aware of. She told about her father and his never-ending quest to eradicate the diseases that had ravaged this part of the world. Small pox had wiped out whole villages in just days. The death toll was almost complete because the people did not want to leave their area to get medical help. It was too difficult for her Father to trek far to bring supplies to the affected villages; therefore, the people just died and the neighboring villages just shunned the area so that the same thing did not happen to them. It was a terrible time and will most likely happen again with some other disease. Sprig continued her-rapid fire dialogue a defense to allay her fears. She told us about her travels up the mountain on this very trail. She had seen the flash of light from my binoculars and was curious enough to begin the climb. Most natives did not have any binoculars so she was encouraged to gain the area with a minimal of apprehension. As she talked, she would occasionally look down at me with a wide, bright smile that gave me erratic heartbeats. I was certain that it didn't mean anything to her but her smile sent me off to a time of daydreaming. Just as my mind was relaxing and coming to interesting parts in my musing, I sensed a sudden halting of our progression.

Down the trail about one hundred yards stood three young men with hands on their hips. If ever there was an observation of young old geezers, they were it. Each had a bow over their shoulders with a quiver attached to their bodies and a spear clenched at their right hand. They were tall, skinny, and more ugly than I remembered from the other night. Sprig was the first to speak.

"What's this all about?"

I was about to answer when Luther interjected, "nothing to worry about young Sprig. I have a pistol with many shots and there are only three of them."

I wondered out loud, "should we wait for them to approach us or should we continue on down the trail?" before anyone answered I followed with a comment that reflected my displeasure of the attentions these three had paid me the other night. "I think we should continue down the trail and see what these three brigands are made of."

Without another word, we began to move forward to meet these evil antagonists. The mule didn't like the situation for one reason or another. He put his head down and his ears up and very hesitantly moved forward at Sprig's persistent urging. We agreed to show some sign of power so we brandished our weapons in the air so they could see and understand the folly of their threatening stance. As we approached, they moved ever so slightly towards the heavy undergrowth indicating hesitancy on their part. When we had arrived at the spot of their threatening, they had melted back into the jungle. This event caused us to stop and ponder our present situation.

"I think we must change what we are now doing. The plane could be ten feet away from this path and we would not even be able to spot it unless our noses indicated fire or burning brush if the plane had caught on fire at impact.

"Sprig, is there another path on higher ground allowing us a better view of the surrounding area?"

"Yes. There is a trail about a mile away that would be on higher ground. It would be hard to get to because of the brush and heavy vegetation. It is on a rise called the Hogback but is a longer trek to the mission."

I volunteered the best plan that I could think of.

"Let's move off this main trail and maybe we can leave the three brigands behind. It will be tough going especially for Bump. I think I have seen a few game trails intersecting with this main one. We must find one of these and start our cross-country trek. Do we have a machete in our outfit?

Sprig pulled out her machete from a scabbard on the flank of Bump and held it high indicating a proclamation of a victor's prize. She is more captivating than a royal queen. She flashed her smile that was complimenting her lovely blue eyes. A site to behold by any suitor but especially me.

It was not long before we found a game trail that was to our liking. We looked back to see if the three were observing us. Seeing no one in sight, we began the arduous task of making a way for Bump to move through the narrow path. Luther was first with the machete, swinging and singing, enjoying the reclamation of a recognizable trail. Bump was not happy. Eventually Sprig had to dismount to facilitate the Mule's progress. This was hard work and hot as the day went on. Luther and I changed places occasionally so that no one person would wear out. Sprig talked to and led her mule to keep the brute moving.

The day wore on with little or no threatening from the underbrush. The vegetation fought back at every turn. We made good progress but we also made frequent stops to drink water and let Luther pass out snacks. We gave Bump some sustenance that Sprig had supplied to keep him happy

Looking at our back trail on a regular basis to be certain that no person was following us, I was pleased to conclude we were alone. The conversations tapered off as the going became much harder. Just when we thought that our new arrangement was turning into some kind of folly, Luther gave a sign of warning. Going around Bump and Sprig I asked Luther what was the reason he called a stop.

He quietly said with a conspiratorial glance around, "I see a vast clearing up head that could be a location of a village."

Sprig was quick to answer. "I think the area is deserted because I have noticed that Bump has not made any moves to indicate any new presence by his ears forward or his muzzle up in the air gathering any strange scents. With this in mind, we advanced as quietly as possible. Luther again took the machete and cut way brush and vegetation as quietly as possible. When we reached the area, we were surprised to see a beautiful extensive savannah that stretched for a mile or more. We came out onto this grassy plain and stopped to take in the view. The savannah lay next to the hogback.

When we climbed up onto the hogback we were able to see for great distances on three sides. With my binoculars, I was able to see a dark spot at the very end of the savannah that melded into the jungle. Could this be the result of a plane crash? We decided that we would travel along the hogback for about an hour when it would be high noon. At that point, we made observations that are more detailed towards the dark spot. The mule was happy to be out of the thick vegetation even with Sprig once more riding on his back.

"Luther, have you an idea for lunch as I am getting hungry."

"Well Dix, since we have a goal ahead I thought a quick repast with a short time for preparations would be sufficient. Does that dark spot appear more like what we have surmised it to be?"

Sprig was surprised at our nonchalant way of dismissing the urgency of reaching the edge of the savannah to determine the existence of the crashed plane.

"Why are you thinking of food at a time like this? I am all for snacking and then to keep moving forward to get the medicines to the mission. We must not stop for trivial reasons to just eat food at a time like this."

Looking me in the eye, she continued with her mild rebuke. "This medicine is very important to Randall and Dad to administer to the local natives. Dickson Straight, I thought you would be most anxious to get the meds and also to retrieve the payroll as quickly as possible."

I was surprised with this tidbit of new information from the lithe and fetching Ms Sprig, "Who is Randall?"

"You know we were sent to find the downed plane and to retrieve what we could and then go on to the mission for further instructions," Luther added with a certainty that it would sidetrack my inquiry about Randall. "We can snack while we advance if old Bump is willing," said Luther as an addendum.

We slowed down as Luther passed out the requested snacks and we complimented the food with water from our individual canteens.

Soon after this, Luther began to complain about his toothache.

I've champed down too hard on some of this jerky and now my tooth is giving me fits.

"I don't have anything for pain," offered up Sprig with gestures towards her saddlebags.

"I guess you will have to just tough it out," was my comment.

All the time we were involved in these diversions we had advanced to the point where we could see with our naked eyes the dark spot near the edge of the savannah. It was a wreckage of some kind. We were still not able to determine if it was a plane, maybe a vehicle, or even a large hut that had been burned. It might have been set on fire to give it that dark of appearance. Taking out my glass, I gave the area a diligent search. I concluded to the others and myself that the blacken spot was definitely a burned patch that had a pattern that was like a plane, but I saw no debris. With this information, we all pressed on with an urgency of substantial proportions.

The hogback began to move down towards the plateau's level. Bump's ears went up as his muzzle lifted to a new height to indicate a new presence was near. Suddenly out of the bush, a horde of menacing natives appeared in full war paint and intent. This caught us off guard, resulting in out capture. The next few minutes were filled with confusion and fear. No time to acquire our weapons, we placidly surrendered to the overwhelming forces to await our fate. Luther and I were trussed up like pigs going to market, strung on a pole with hands and feet secured to the pole resulting in an upside, brain-hurting position. Something that caused Luther some great discomfort augmented by a toothache. It was hard to see but it looked like Sprig was bound by restraints on her wrists and led forward at the end of a pole. It was not the way we had planned our afternoon discovery of the downed plane.

The trip through the jungle was painful and seemed to be miles long. I could hear Luther grunting and groaning in time with the swaying of his trussed—up body. I was soon in sync with him as we went down an incline. The chanting of the natives added an ethereal quality to this entire confused state. I did not see Sprig but I was certain she was being pushed or pulled right along with the rest of us. After an indeterminably time we came to rest in the center of a compound that was surrounded by little huts. I was relieved to see upon my neck-straining scan that no giant pot was boiling over a hot fire. Women came out of their huts and began to poke us with sticks and stones. Names will never hurt you, but these sticks and stones surely caused a lot of unnecessary pain. After the fun had died down, we were untied and cast into a hovel that pigs had been living or just existing. The smell and conditions were intolerable. In this pen both Luther and I could at least converse. Unable to effectively close our noses, we talked, breathing through our mouths

"I just saw them take our Sprig into a large hut where an assembly has gathered." I went on. "My hope and prayers are that Sprig might talk some sense into this bunch. I think we could use a small miracle about now. What is your take on all this?"

Luther, never at a loss for words replied with some sarcastic remarks.

These people are biting the hand that ministers to them. I am sure the good doctor has been to this place sometime to help the sick and dying. They should be rejoicing and preparing the fatted calf for us, with rings on our fingers and gold armbands."

"Just pray the good Lord has an interest in our predicament and will cause a happy and quick conclusion." My two cents worth was unnecessary as I noticed Luther bowing his head with lips moving. He had beaten me to the punch this time.

After a while, all of the chatter had subsided in the big hut as the night began to creep into the compound only making the situation appear darker. We both continued to rub our wrists and ankles trying to get them to recover. We both commented that no pigs were in residence causing us to speculate that the natives had run out of food. This thought only threw light on the probabilities that we might become a meal in the near future for hungry natives. When we had sunk to the lowest possibilities of our rescue, a great hue and cry came from the assembly. Out came Sprig on the shoulders of shouting, boisterous men heading towards the pigpen. In only minutes, we were freed and taken to a river to clean up the smell and dirt of the day. On the way, Sprig informed us that when she revealed to them she was the daughter of the mission doctor and you were my friends and companions, they were only too glad to set us all free with a banquet to follow. Luther's only comment was, "finally." His lips still moved giving thanks no doubt to the God of mercy and helps in time of trouble.

What a relief to be free once again and clean to boot. We reminded our selves of the urgency of our mission but Sprig cautioned us not to offend these people's gestures of good will of a banquet.

"Maybe we can cut short the festivities by telling the merrymakers that we are on a mission for the doctor and time was of the essence," I said with as much wisdom I could muster for my voice and face.

Sprig scrunched up he nose in a way that indicted an unsavory task ahead was hers.

"One must be careful and use what tact one could bring to the discourse," replied the dutiful Ms Sprig.

"Maybe we could stay for the first part as it is too dark to venture on," offered Luther. No doubt, he was thinking of his stomach that was in need of filling.

"I concur with you both, just be gentle and emphasize the need to continue on early in the morning if that seems right with you," I added to the conversation. Sprig was up to the task as she gently informed the headman of our need to leave early in the morning.

The festivities were not raucous but lengthy. The people went on into the night so far that the three of us dozed off only to find ourselves stiff and cranky when the morning crept into the compound. They had left us sleeping and gone off to their individual huts to sleep in when they expended all of their energies in rejoicing.

Sprig was on her feet and looking around in expectation. Her face blossomed into a smile as she noticed that on the far side of the compound an old man was coming towards us. As he was advancing, Sprig related to us she had asked some tribesmen to accompany us to the crash site and on to the mission, last night. When the old man had reached us, Sprig asked him in his native tongue if some young men would be coming with us to show us the way and protect us from any further complications. The old man replied in English to our surprise. "No one will escort you further into the jungle. Our Shaman has decreed that the great noise and fire with much black smoke was now an evil place, inhabited by evil spirits of all kinds. No tribesman will travel with you on this dangerous and fruitless endeavor."

Sprig was saddened but tried not to show it as she thanked the old man profusely. Luther and I both looked blankly as the thoughts of us going back into that jungle with many other natives unhappy with the white man and his interventions, excluding medical help.

With that information under our belts, we retrieved our backpacks and headed back into the jungle with some trepidation. The mule was still with us as he had enjoyed some friendly ministrations from the natives, as they had not been exposed to any mules before. With replenished supplies, we would be able to spend a long time without having to look for food or wood. Our weapons had been returned with empty cylinders or magazines. Now all I had to do was to find out more about Randall. Other than that, we were set to face the day's new challenges, we thought. The three scalawags were still on all of our minds.

CHAPTER THREE

T HE JUNGLE WITH its foreboding mass of vegetation began to slap us in the face. This would of course bring us tears and irritation of the eyes to an extent that our vision was impaired. Luther once again, the gallant gentleman, went first with the machete to clear a path that was more passable than the faint game trail we had chosen. The old man back at the compound had indicted this game trail would lead us towards the great loud sound and smoke that we surmised was a crashed airplane.

Not far from the village, we came to a place that showed the remnants of a light airplane. The scorched earth gave no clues as to the pilot's destiny or his whereabouts. Searching through the debris, we found nothing further to support that the pilot survived the crash. The money was gone as well as the supply of medicines or drugs. We surmised local natives had taken every thing, including bones back to their village to show the surrounding villages what could happen to them if they harmed or attacked the village with the white man's remains. This was a gruesome conclusion to our search for the plane and pilot. We now had to get back to the mission so that we could give our full attention to my map and the place marked X.

We began our journey towards the mission after a short interval. So with heavy hearts and a sense of loss we headed in the direction that Sprig and our compass gave us. Luther once more took the lead with his singing machete in this jungle of springy branches and pricking vines of a tenacious nature. The going was laborious but fruitful as we soon found a better trail that gave Bump more room to negotiate the serpentine trail that also went up and down. Ravines and hillocks were the order of the day. The day began to warm up quickly as we made our way down this game trail to who knows where? We passed many monkeys and an assortment of grazing animals, warthogs, and occasionally mysterious noises in the underbrush that made Bump very nervous and jumpy. Bump wanted to stop and graze a little himself and to drink some water in a small stream we had found. The afternoon rains came on time with its usual cooling down before it all turned to a muggy, humid, sauna. The annoying insects took a short respite while we luxuriated in the final showers of the day. The trail became very muddy and slippery. The packs on the mule were protected by waterproof covering so we had one less problem to worry about.

When the rain stopped, the jungle became a virtual cacophony of symphonic insect pandemonium. The noise was so loud one tried to cover the ears for relief. This gesture was to no avail. Bump was more annoyed by the abundance of little biting, stinging, and nuisances all over his hide trying to find a place to disturb. Sprig was making a valiant effort to ward off the little irritants.As we were coping with these little annoyances, it caused us to drop our guard for external dangers. In only seconds, we were surrounded by a covey of angry and menacing tribal pygmies. With spears and knives, they made known their apparent supremacy in numbers and weapons. No time for any counter offensive as our hands were being bound in a practiced flurry of activity in seconds. They all seemed less tense with Sprig since she was not bound or tormented by the excited company over capturing three white trespassers.

The journey to 'who knows where,' took us down faint trails and darkened underbrush. Leading Bump first in line gave some relief to the swatting branches in our faces. With our hands bound, we had no defense from these constantly scratching whips from the low vegetation.

It seemed like hours before we heard a scattering of high pitched voices coming from what I surmised was the waiting village with its new and more severe punishments. The village must know we are coming and they are preparing a welcoming reception. Poor Luther was dealing with his toothache and gave extra vocal noises of pain and discomfort. At this point, he was getting sick and validated it by way of copious amounts of regurgitated substance. This event caused the little people extra voice and excitement for no reason other than his discomfiture. We had walked this far many times before but I think the heat and hurt had taken its toll on our friend my colleague, Luther Locke. Multiple pain relievers didn't help his stomach. Sprig by hook or crook, came to his aid with word of comfort and a wet handkerchief to his fevered brow. The pygmies seem to allow this show of regard towards one of the prisoners. Coming into the captor's living compound we were met by a group of females making all kinds of noises that were suppose to scare or challenge the group of prisoners.

Once again, Sprig was treated with some kindness, for what reason I was not certain. Poor Luther continued his moans and cries of pain even though the journey had ended. I kept my eyes on Sprig for more than one reason. She was our only hope for escaping this dilemma. Sprig was trying to converse with some of the screaming women, hoping to catch someone's attention. Eventually some females received Sprig as an equal to discuss the present situation with some calmness and decorum. The little knot was quite animated with hand pointing with accompanied waves and gestures of the most intense nature. One moment Sprig seemed to be making progress and the in the next she was trying to make peace with the group. The entire scene was accentuated by the continued harassment of Luther and I. Luther grimaced often as the pain came and went with him, as his toothache was still first on his agenda of coping with pain even though the females happily poked us with sticks.

My mind went back to the start of the search and it all seemed to be rather petty now in the shadow as our present possible fatal circumstance. It loomed to make life a very real and desirable alternative to finding X. All my musings ended as I viewed what was happening around me. I wasn't frightened but I was chagrined as the gathering took on an ugly mood.

CHAPTER FOUR

THE PYGMIES ALL gathered around Luther, as his groans became a mystery when they had not hurt him or caused him any bloody wounds since arriving in the compound. Like any investigator, the little men poked and pushed at Luther trying to find the spot that was causing him to moan and groan. Since they did not meet with success, they began to dance about him with boisterous threatening and more severe jabbing to evoke the kind of groan and moan they were accustomed to. This entire spectacle now viewed by the females with jaundiced eye. They had befriended Sprig with hand dialogue and halting languages. They now viewed the scene with some disapproval occasioned by the hurling of small bits of debris at their men. It was a comical scene.

Not so comical was the great pot beginning to boil over its blazing fire. The pygmies stopped harassing Luther to begin to throw into the pot various chunks of vegetables, herbs, or spices. The coup de grace' was when I noticed what appeared to be an antelope hindquarter thrown into pot. This was indicating to me that the meat for the stew was not white meat. A happy event I thought.

While all of this was going on the females were regaling the men to listen to them. Evidently, Sprig had gotten through to some of the women as she had done with the other tribes' people, earlier. When some of the men listened to their wives, they only made more noise and danced around the compound with a great furiousness that was almost frightening. We all noticed that they avoided the plane's artifacts that stood at one end the compound like so many painfully unappreciated idols. When all the excitement died down Sprig was allowed to come to Luther and I to tell us of her success in describing by signs who we where and what we doing in the jungle. In a very short time, we found ourselves released from our bonds. This allowed us to walk around and smile at all the little females that had obtained our freedom after harassing us with pointy sticks

Sprig related to us that she had convinced the tribe that we meant only good and would cast out the devils that might still exist in the fire pit where they collected the plane's artifacts. She also conveyed the truth about the medical supplies helping others to get well from diseases and maladies. "In their telling they revealed to me that some of the plane's spirit waste was in a special hut, they had constructed to house it so that the spirits would not harm them. I would like to go there to see what exactly is in that hut." With Sprig leading the way with only one old woman as her protector, the three of us approached a hastily constructed hut of Lilliputian dimensions. Stooping to enter the hut we are could barely fit inside the structure. The old Pygmy female stayed outside chanting a pitiful sound of warning and sorrow. As our eyes became accustomed to the dark interior, we were all relieved to that it contained several containers of medical supplies. Upon closer examination, the sack of money was positioned in the middle of the stack.

No doubt, this was to negate its harmful power according to all of the sounds and gestures presented us recently by the wee folk of the jungle.

"Let's grab this stuff and get out of here as fast as we can," said Luther.

Sprig was not in agreement when she offered her counsel. "Let us just stay calm and move slowly so as not to alarm or disquiet our hosts. We can do this in a casual way so that we are not a threat to them." I could see that her wisdom was far beyond her years. We followed her advice, brought out the supplies slowly, and headed for the mule. A host of young admirers surrounded old Bump. I was unable to determine if it was the oddity of the beast or that she represented many fine cuts of meat. We set off in the bush with exciting memories.

CHAPTER FIVE

LEAVING THE SMALL people's village we splashed and slashed through the jungle making enough noise to alert any wild dangerous animals or peoples for we sounded like a herd of elephants. Sprig was telling us that the mission was located several miles from this place we now occupied. How she knew I did not know. She had indicated that some of the landmarks told her that the mission was straight ahead. "I think I have been in this area once or twice. A river is just over that thick stand of trees. We can follow the river from there, if you want to. It may save us some time instead of using this trail. Our Medical mission is on the banks of that river. We call it the Sadly River because we have noticed so many bodies floating down its waters."

Making our way over towards the place Sprig had indicated we came across a valley instead of a river. "We are lost," she said.

"How far off base are we Sprig?" Luther's voice almost cracked with emotion as he viewed the great valley below us. His stomach was over reacting.

Sprig began to tear-up with her eyes producing a stream of hot salty liquid.

"I was so certain that this was a place my father and Randall had come to several years ago on a mission of mercy to help some non-native German ranchers."

"Randall told me to look for some markers to remember the place in case I ever came this way again. The large group of trees gave me a certainty that this was the place."

"Well it looks like this Randall didn't give you enough markers to be sure of your position," I said with a little bit of rancor in my comment.

Luther gave out his assessment at this seemingly dilemma.

"We have food and water and strength to go on and find this place without wasting time here."

We made our way down through briars and brambles until we came to a ledge overlooking the valley below. Our troubles were turned into triumphant cries of discovery as the ledge revealed the river below the ledge that had hid itself from our view earlier.

"I told you a river was just over the trees," said a joyous Sprig with a satisfied smile on her radiant face. Now all we have to do is follow the river upstream to the mission grounds."

Carefully threading our way down and around the ledge we finally got to the river and its heavily vegetative banks. Just as we started up the river on the near bank, a tumult of deafening screaming human forms presented themselves in the form of a small band of slave runners from the Middle East. They descended on us even before Bump could have given a warning. With a rapidly rarely seen in this part of the world we found ourselves bound and trussed up like animals going to that the place of final proceedings.

Hopping along on bound feet, they soon discovered that my falling down and requiring assistance to get up was not very economical. Luther was having the same kind of difficulty. Sprig walked normally behind the Mule in a subservient manner but spewing verbal statements of the most deflating or bruising kind. It didn't contain any bad words. Her verbal barrage did not deter our captors to relent or to repent. The chatter of these men constituted a never-ending sound of bragging and boasts. I continued to wonder if their vocal cords would wear out. Sprig also would fit that category with some left over for Luther and me.I was surprised to see our three skinny thieves of earlier encounters off occupying the bush, secretly. They might have been scouting earlier for the slave catching Brigands to locate easy prey of an exceptional quality. They never joined the slavers, though. The slavers looked at us with the faces of victorious, cruel antagonists. These Arabic looking people displayed their penchant to capture desirable slave material and sell them to awaiting criminal malcontents. A Harem might be the projected place for my Sprig, thought I.

I soon received a relief, as my feet felt a reprieve when the captors untied them. Luther received the same generous gesture. This present predicament was as dangerous as any we had encountered previously. These folks would not be talked out of the precious cargo they had captured.

The group took us about a mile down stream before stopping us to be loaded on to a small craft. Herded onto the boat, we three waited patiently for the next calamity to descend down around our ears. Bump's fate caused him to follow a small remnant back into the jungle with his precious cargo intact. Why?

The leaders appropriated the medical supplies and payroll still on Bump. I had looked and noticed that only a few bandits took much time to evaluate the medical boxes or the moneybag, acting nonchalantly. I wondered if that were so, it was likely only a scant number of the brigands would share in the booty. The rest would continue to practice their devilment living the life of perpetual fools. The three amigos had melted back into the jungle.

My head was swimming with visions of our escape and retrieving the supplies and payroll. The visions all ended with the realization that this was not a dreamy situation but a predicament that would require great ingenuity and daring. My hope was that Luther and Sprig also were viewing the situation with an eye towards escape. Looking at the crew, I became aware that only five slavers were guarding us and maneuvering the boat.

The boat was small and reeked of misuse and deterioration. It was ill equipped with oars and sails. The sails were torn and raggedy. The oars had seen better days. My guess is that the boat represented a stolen prize from some poor, inattentive people a long time ago. The hope in my mind came to be that it would last a little while longer. The craft creaked and groaned like a dying giant with arthritis.

My first thought was to try to communicate with Luther and Sprig without words. We had tried some conversation earlier but whiplashes resulted in our attempt. I noticed that Sprig was crying gently with soft sobs. Her face exhibited a puffiness and flush that gave her a real sense of vulnerability not seen before by me. It was a noble trait in my mind that one so vibrant and expressive could also be passive and yet so beautiful at the same time.

Seeing my stare, Sprig managed to give me the faintest of smiles to sooth my aching heart and hands. Luther, the fighter, was deep in thought as he looked up to the two of us. His face was set in a powerful way to indicate he had thought of something positive concerning our imprisonment. His eyes traveled to the man on watch moving his head in way to suggest the first order of business. Having received the suggestion, I nodded in approval. Sprig tipped her head to the two men on the rail talking and smoking. I lifted up my feet in a gesture of bolting towards them to cause a falling overboard of the two captors. Luther mouthed the word three meaning to execute on the count of three. Sprig shook here head in disapproval by nodded towards the hold where two unaccounted men most likely existed, probability asleep or drunk. The smell of strong drink wafted up from the hold in copious quantity. My thought was to close the hatch as we engaged the three men on deck. I tried to mouth the words so Luther could comprehend my action as best I could. He nodded in agreement.

Therefore, the plan was for me to close the hatch to keep two of the men disabled while Luther rose up and bumped two of the rail huggers into the river. Sprig accepted the task to disable the steersman and somehow with her body, force him to the deck and tromp him into submission. With muted smiles on all of our faces, we in unison sprang into action to defeat our foes and free our selves of this malignant circumstance. I was sure this would be a moment to remember all of our lives, if we lived.

CHAPTER SIX

THE EFFORT MUST be in proportion to the circumstances. Luther was the first out of the box after mouthing three. He projected as a rugged sort of fellow with hair askew and eyes blazing with the look of an athlete ready to score at the expense of the opposing team. Sprig also had the look of a winner as she sprang forward to execute her part in the escape plan. I moved towards the hatch to shut it as Sprig disabled the steersman. Luther was at ease as his bulk easily caused the two rail huggers to fall overboard with a pleasant soft sound of perfection. Sprig was on top of the steersman using her feet to pummel the surprised and frightened brigand. I had a tough time closing the hatch, as it was old and slightly sticky. With a great heave, I was able to get it shut before the two below had a chance to respond. The entire scene had the speed and rhythm of a hushed course ballet. Luther and I had to stand on the hatch door to give weight and security for the attempts of the two below trying to gain access to the deck. While in this position Sprig began to untie our bonds after rendering the steersman unconscious.

With hands untied, we completed our ability to act. Our next job was to secure the boat as our own. The steersman found himself being thrown overboard. We were glad that his weight was slight. The two under classmen waited a similar fate. Their sounds indicated inebriation of the medium range. As I opened the hatch they came out, one by one as Luther used a belay pin to render them incapable of any shenanigans. The boat drifted back towards the bank allowing us to deposit the two unconscious slavers on the bank. Sprig was now the steersman handling the craft with some latent talent.

"Now that we are free from this group I am thinking we should abandon the boat and start back upstream to reach the mission before anything else happens," said Sprig as she wiped away water that had splashed on her.

"I suppose the mule, medical supplies, and payroll are destined to being lost to the slavers," said Luther with a touch of sarcasm.

I was quick to add, "If we thought we could recover them with a minimum of difficulty I think we should, and right away."

"Well, I know all of those things are important to my father and Randall but I don't want to risk life and limb for things that could be replaced. We have been very fortunate so far. In another couple of weeks more supplies would be sent in and the payroll loss was already producing havoc with the miners so a few days wouldn't change things."

"That may be true but I have lost a treasure map that was packed into the supply bag. I have risked life and limb to keep that map as an adventure after we returned the supplies and payroll. Now it belongs to a bunch of brigands and slavers, denying us to find a fortune."

"You surely don't think you have a real treasure map for this area. There have been hundreds of phony maps sold here to unsuspecting tourists. Randall was ready to buy one when he first came into the area. Dad says that only fools and rich people buy treasure maps."

"I still think we can go back down the river, and subdue these miscreants and retrieve the supplies and payroll. Luther and I are a formidable force when properly utilized, and you Sprig, would add immensely to the faction resulting in a certain victory."

"I am almost convinced after the way we took over the boat without even one causality on our part. I guess we can go and try to recover what is ours. The worst thing that could happen would be we were killed."

With this comforting confirmation of agreement, we three exited the boat; taking only some wooden belay pins for protection and one knife, we had removed from the old steersman. The task before us seemed to be daunting but doable with surprise and stealth on our side.

The boat struck sand but we pushed it back into the river to make it difficult for others to use it to our disadvantage later. The night had fallen during our recent escapade. This made it difficult to impossible to find a clear track to follow. Luther led the way, using the knife from time to time to help clear a way for Sprig and myself. The night sounds were ominous and scary. Bugs that hid from the noonday sun come out at night, to take a vengeance on all who venture out, not wearing proper clothing.

The progress was slow but reassuring, as Luther had found some indication of a trail that ran close to the river noticeable by the slaver's recent passing. His advance was partly due to a moon that peeked out on occasion to avoid sticky and prickly branches attempting to take back the trail. Many were already broken from the advance of Bump and the slavers up ahead.

I began to tell Luther of my plan to try to find the treasure that the map indicated. Sprig's negative comments about the folly of buying treasure maps from old men in a jungle bar had not deterred my desire to continue the search, even after reaching the mission.

His only response in a casual manner was, "I have some candy and a pack of gum still in my cargo pants where the miscreants had not searched. Do you want some?" Sprig was also included in this generous gesture.

My reply was in the affirmative. The area had rained every afternoon so we could get some water from a collection in some stumps. I passed some of the candy bar to Sprig. She smiled in a most appreciative manner. We paused at intervals to fortify our bodies with the stump water. After Sprig finished her candy, she began to tell of other sources of nourishment in the jungle.

"If we could find a large rotting log I could rummage around the debris and find some nice juicy grubs. A small fire and we could have a tasty treat eating the crispy protein rich grubs."

Luther responded immediately. "I'm all for it. I'm so hungry I feel weak. The candy didn't help very much and the gum is not keeping its taste," as he passed around some more gum.

The night wore on. We all were moving forward as fast as we could, considering all of the ill fortune besetting us. We had passed the place were our abduction took place. Moving down the river valley was of the highest priority to reach the other brigands and Bump. Before morning, we gained the site that Bump and his captors made a camp. At this point, all of us moved with more verve and alacrity. It became difficult for Sprig to keep up with Luther and myself. I could hear her huffing and puffing with some soft groans thrown in for good measure. With a soft but firm voice, I whispered to Lunch Box, "let's slow down so we will not wear out before catching up with thieves."

"That may not be necessary," he replied softly.

"I thought I had smelled some smoke earlier and then saw a flicker of light up ahead."

This revelation caused all of us to stop and take inventory of our resources. A plan of action now is of an absolute necessity. Our only means of attack consisted of a knife and a belay pin from the boat.

"Why do you think the slavers have stopped so near their departure," asked Sprig.

"My guess is that they wanted to tally up the booty, and celebrate with some liquid refreshments no doubt carried by them for just such an occasion."

"I wonder what they did with Bump. He has been a real blessing around the mission. I not only feel responsible for him but I have come to appreciate all the things he has done for the mission and me. These kinds of slavers think of him only meat on the end of a skewer for a feast."

"Let's not worry about that now. We need to sneak up on them to find a way to subdue them," whispered Luther as he motioned us to move forward at a slower and stealth-like posture. We came upon the brigand's camp a short time later. All six of them we found laying around a dying campfire in an apparent result of too much celebration with white lightening. It was with hand motions that Luther took the belay pin and moved forward to tap each slaver on the head to help them sleep longer and better. The scene was almost comical as we three moved forward on tiptoe to accomplish a neutralizing of these miscreants. One by one, Luther applied the belay pin in such a manner to help the slavers into a long but painful sleep when awakening.

Chapter Seven

W HEN WE WERE certain all of the slavers were busy napping we began to scout around for our packs and other supplies. Sprig was tramping around the perimeter to try and locate Bump. Luther found our packs and the medical supplies. The payroll moneybag was also located with some of the money stuffed in the pockets of the sleeping beauties.

"Hey guys I found old Bump over here in this little glen just enjoying himself by cropping the grass. He seems unfazed about his dire circumstance in the hands of the brigands. His plight only caused him to dine furiously on this glen's green grass." Sprig brought Bump into the camp area with an air of victory. She then noticed that the fire had some grubs roasting on the spit over the small blaze.

"I can see we can eat some protein before we take off again. They look toasty brown, just right for the pickings."

"Come on Sprig, We can certainly find some munchies in our packs even though their contents are strewn all over the campsite," said Luther eyeing the grubs with jaundiced eye.

I continued to inventory the surrounding contents, both theirs and ours giving out verbally my findings.

"The medical supplies are intact, except the injectables. They look like the sleepers had tried to drink them, no doubt hoping for alcohol. They are either outdated or contaminated making them useless. The money bag has seen better days but it will still be capable to deliver to the miners or their bosses."

"I think dad or Randall have radioed the center for a delivery to the mission by now."

"If this is the case we can ease up on our drive to get to the mission at a fast pace," Luther offered with a slight relief in his voice.

I was not convinced; "we should not forget the roving miners with malice on their minds to do-in anyone that represents authority or the American way."

"I have not noticed the three miscreants that were with the slavers earlier. They also were my antagonists at the jungle bar. They are nowhere in sight now. Moving out of here should still with care and diligence."

"Dix is correct. We must still move with all care and stealth through these last jungle miles before we reach the mission on this river. Our direction is upstream where more unknowns exist," said Sprig with hope in her voice and face.

I was pleased that Sprig heard my counsel and agreed, with a smile that could toast old bread into new. We decided it would be best if we ate a little then began our trek upriver to the mission, posthaste.

Trying the little roasted grubs reminded me of crispy fries and they crunched with a satisfying sound. We soon devoured all of the slaver's grubs and looked around for more. Sprig had put on water for coffee. In our backpacks, we found our dried fruit was still edible. The thieves might not have known what they were. They rejected them like some of our other goodies. With hot coffee and other nourishments in our bodies, we all felt satisfied as well as fueled for what lay ahead. The sleepers were still napping when we left their camp. Old Bump seemed happy to be with Sprig once again. He accepted all of our kit and caboodle with an ease that was honed by years of being a beast of burden. He and Sprig were in the middle of our little caravan keeping up with Luther who was in the lead.

Our progress was impressive as the various landmarks we had passed earlier, melted like hot butter. The trail was more familiar on our return up river so that our observations became as keen as a high priced private eye not having to look at the trail as often. The river meandered quite a lot trying to get us lost or off trail. Once or twice, we had to back track to get our bearings adjusted. The traveling went on through most of the day, stropping only to rest and nibble a few bites of food. We moved with a determination that would have pleased a drill sergeant. Bump was still full of vim and vinegar as the day began to wan. Coming into a clearing hurriedly, a place we had not visited before, we stopped to experience the surroundings. The air had a feeling of danger crawling up my spine a tingly manner. "HAVE YOU EVER FELT SOMEONE WAS WATCHING YOU WHEN NO ONE WAS IN SIGHT?" I murmured out loud. I heard a twang as well as a thud followed by a scream of pain coming from my colleague and friend. Looking at Luther I saw one arrow sticking awkwardly from his side. The feathers on the arrow were the same that had been used to attack us back at the climbing wall. I pulled my revolver that I retrieved from the slavers and shot in the direction I thought the arrow came. No sound came from the brush. Sprig was already at

Luther's side trying to determine the extent of the wound. My first impression was to run to the brush where I thought the shooter had hidden but was pulled back by the very reasonable influence of Sprig.

"They will have vacated that area in only seconds," came the voice of logic.

Sprig was hunched down with Luther behind a small bush trying to minister to Luther's impaled side. Luther added his concern "Let's get this arrow out before it kills me. Sprig agreed, as she viewed the wound with concern written all over her face. "We must remove this arrow since I have noticed some poison dipped on the tip to render the recipient a paralyzing or deathly blow."

She authoritatively continued, "It would be a help to make a small fire and boil some water. This wound needs cleansing and the application of hot compresses to try and neutralize the poison."

I took this to be my clue to gather wood and build a fire to boil the water. This I accomplished in short order. During this time, Sprig had gently removed the arrow and its tip since it had not been imbedded very deep. Luther managed a few comments about what we might cook over my small fire. The water was hot that Sprig applied with a soft cloth accompanied by Lunch Box's controlled wails of pain and discomfort. While the fire, still glowed hot, I put on the pot for coffee. Soon the rich aroma found its way to Luther, who commented, "how about some of that brew along with any pain medicine in the supplies?"

Sprig was already searching through the medical supplies for pain tablets and healing salves. She found them and gave them to Luther to use as she instructed him. With hot coffee in his cup and jerky in his hand, Luther seemed to be at ease. Sprig was not going to let the fire go out without providing us with some pan-fried bread to go with the coffee. She made the bread and fried it in the pan. It smelled delicious after being on short rations for several days. With a flurry that looked magical, she produced some honey to go with the bread. It was a very special time for the three of us. All of this time we kept a wary eye on the area where we had thought the arrow came from. The three thieves of jungle bar fame might be in the vicinity with diabolical harm in mind. It would fall to me to make a more extensive search in that area to determine if the threat was still present. Checking my gun for shells, I took off in that direction.

"I'll be back in a few minutes after I take a look around for any antagonists still in the area."

After a careful search with my thirty-eight at the ready, I found no evidence of threats to us. On my return, I was surprised to notice Luther building a great sweat on his forehead. Sprig had also noticed it, declaring that Luther was running a fever. His Side also was beginning to look purple or gray. She ordered Luther to lie down as we both covered him with a blanket and his outer clothing that we had removed earlier.

Sprig was a very attentive nurse as she applied cold cloths to Luther's feverish brow every five or six minutes from a pail of water I had brought from the river. "I think this fever will last until tomorrow morning. We had best make our camp for the night right here. I will just keep putting cold compresses on Luther while you make certain no one comes with terror in mind during the night." Sprig was adamant, as she got comfortable next to Lunch Box for the vigil that lay ahead. Luther got all the attention while all I got was the pail to get more water for Sprig. Dickson Straight relegated to water boy. Only for my queen would I subject myself for this duty.

CHAPTER EIGHT

Luther spent a very fitful night even as Sprig continued her ministrations and compresses. The fever seemed to be minimal but the poison had taken effect by exaggerated muscle spasms and twitching.I had gone into the forest for quite a ways and found no sign of anyone hiding or leaving any telltale sign. Breakfast was hearty and fulfilling as Sprig had miraculously prepared food and hot drinks while still keeping an attentive eye on her charge. The food rations were getting low. Sprig did not reveal this to us but I could tell that the stores had begun to dwindle; no doubt because of our vigorous appetites or possible some one has slipped into camp and removed some of our supplies. This new thought became to wallow around my mind to the extent that I began to devise a kind of trap for any surreptitious or unauthorized withdrawals of our provisions. While Sprig was busy with her assigned tasks, I set a trap by bending a young sapling to the ground and rigging it with a trip wire. I would make sure our food sack was set in a position so that if anyone or any thing approached the food with nefarious intent, the trap would spring and catch the thief. The trap was expertly laid.

The rest of the day was one of keeping a close watch on Luther's condition. We had an ample supply of various medicines but one still worried being so far from civilization. We had decided we could not move until Luther was well enough to walk and carry his pack or able to ride old bump without falling off. The fever had finally broken by nightfall but the poison still seemed to have a muscular grip on Luther's body. We prayed and talked positive to Lunch Box, keeping up his spirits, even though it was difficult to tell if he comprehended all that was going on around him.

Sprig and I keep up the fire to ward off any nosy critters, since we had heard grunting and other animals appearing quite close by, earlier. I had carefully placed the food sack in the range of the trip trap. During this interlude, Sprig took some time off to sit around the cozy fire and wanted to talk. I of course accommodated her with attentive eyes and an interested countenance. I think my proposal of couple of days ago must be setting in with some inquisitiveness.

"Dix, what are you going to do when we return to civilization?"

"I suppose I will go back home and get a job and try to settle down."

She was waiting for another question to ask me. One that any young person must ask himself or herself or even someone they think will be a serious friend.

"Where do you see yourself in five more years or maybe even ten."

This penetrating inquiry would reveal a lot about a person. Their dreams and aspirations would be revealed by this answer more than a lot of guesswork. I knew the worst answer would be; "I don't know." This girl wanted a future with some one that was definite and decisive. Up to now my life had revolved around trips, adventures, excursions, and such like. I would certainly have to level with Sprig if I was to continue to court her. Lies, innuendoes, half-truths had no place in a commitment we both had in the back of our minds. This desire of mine was far more than physical, even though Sprig was a vision to behold on all counts. Her courage and intelligence impressed me as well as her ability to be patient in all kinds of circumstances that I had witnessed on this little trip. I was beginning to warm up to an all-revealing answer when suddenly a cry was heard in the vicinity of the trip trap. This interruption gave Sprig a start and she had immediately taken a stance with her cudgel for a defensive maneuver.

Reaching the trip trap, we saw a young boy who was still clutching in his hands the food sack as a triumphant prize. The trip had caught his leg and threw him off balance and upside down in the air. Sprig came close to understand the boy's cries of surprise and anguish.

"This scamp says he is a displaced person who was very hungry. He also says his little village was pillaged by the roaming unpaid miners of the big copper mine. The miners came into his village looking for food and other comforts. He was driven from the compound out of fear and just ran and ran until he spied our smoke from the fire. He had stayed close by for food unable to hunt or fish because of his hurried departure and exhaustion. He 's such a chatterbox I think we should get him down for more information."Reaching back for my hunting knife I prepared to cut down our youthful intruder. The boy, seeing my knife made another ear shattering screech, because he thought I was going to finish him off, like he had seen others in the jungle meet their afterlife at the end of machetes or knives. When he saw that I cut the trip wire, he was very quiet, demonstrating his acceptance of his fate.

Sprig immediately asked his name and in halting English, he was able to say "Monty."

"This was his name to foreigners," said Sprig. "His real name he did not offer to reveal. I do not want to press the issue."

"Well, Monty what news can you bring to us concerning the marauding miners?"

With stilted English, the lad began a story of fear and trepidation that captured the heart of Sprig to the extent that she began to push food at the young boy with maternal care and regard. The lad was famished and weak so that his dialogue was not only difficult to understand but was the quintessence of brevity. When he stopped, asking for more lemonade that Sprig had whipped up, he pointed to my revolver and stated, "that will keep us safe."

All of the time we were in discussions with Monty, Luther was beginning to exhibit calm muscles and a rerun to normalcy. It was joy to hear him shout,"hey you guys, what's going on over there?"

With this bit of good news I returned to the place where Luther was recuperating, leaving Sprig to care for Monty. Kneeling close to the near normal Lunch Box, I related all that had happened in the hours he was in fever and cleansing the poison from his system. The only remnant of that ill-fated encounter was a gray splotch on his side where the arrow had penetrated. He was more interested in the new arrival and his tales of the past few days than his wound. Food was also on his mind.

'If what he says is true we have a new set of antagonists to avoid as well as prepare for any eventuality."

"Well, your first order of business is to rest awhile longer and get back your strength and vim and vigor. We will talk of eventualities soon enough when you are in tip top condition."

"I know I am now but I could rest just a little to clear my head and get up off this pallet. "You just lie back down and close your eyes so your can recuperate quickly so that we can get on with our trek back up river to the mission compound."After Luther took my counsel, I left to find Sprig and Monty in serious discussions.

"You people are so engrossed in you conversations that I must assume it involves all of our options on how to continue without a confrontation with any marauding, disgruntled, miners."

"Monty was telling me, in his halting English, that the miners have trashed the mine and returned to their home villages, mad as a shark losing his dinner with a sore tooth. This will mean we must avoid any of the several villages between here and the mission. Monty wants us to try and return him safely to his village, later."

Monty was not to be left out of the conversation.

"Me think me can take you around the bad villages."

Sprig was quick to agree as she had early on placed a lot of confidence in this young scamp that had stolen some of our foodstuffs. I figured Sprig must have a plethora of experience here in the bush with the mission dealing with native folks all the time. She had those penetrating eyes that saw more than just your face it was as though she could look inside your soul to reveal the truth. I must remember that. We agreed on this course of action and would leave this place early the next morning.

Monty was very adept at constructing a hammock to spend the night. His strength was returning fast after the copious amounts of food that Sprig fed him. Most of the materials he retrieved from his jungle hid-away. He also gathered more vegetation to make a lean-to for Sprig. Luther and I slept in the tent this night. The afternoon showers would soon appear. Only minutes later the showers came very gently and of short duration. After the shower, Sprig followed Monty partway into the jungle to get Bump and make certain he was fed and watered. That old mule was near where Monty had hidden him near his little space and looked like he was tethered at a place of ample browse close to a little trickle of water. Monty approached the mule and talked to Bump in a caring and knowing way. This boy must have taken care of Bump because we had neglected Bump's essentials while worrying over Luther's arrow wound and the unexpected incursion of its author. When these two came back to camp, they gave a good report on Bump. Final touches were completed on the little lean-to. Sprig was fascinated with her compact abode. Her oohs and ahs were probably for the benefit of the young ears of Monty for his ceaseless endeavors to please Sprig. I volunteered for the first watch with the understanding that when I was ready I would wake up Sprig or Monty for the next watch. Sprig entered her lean-too and Monty his hammock to sleep or rest for the next day's rigors. During my watch, the only human sounds were noticed when Luther either snored or turned over with sounds of discomfort. I heard no sounds from the jungle forest that appeared to be threatening as I had kept the fire burning brightly. The night was warm and conducive to nodding off. Sleep finally took hold of me as I was awakened by Monty giving me a gentle shake. I opened my eyes in an embarrassed way looking into Monty's serious eyes that reflected both disappointment and a seriousness not seen before.

"Mr. Straight, why are you sleeping? I hear far off noises that could be a group of men beating the bush, looking for animals to eat or men to beat."

Monty's poetic warning was taken to be serious for this lad had ears that could hear a fly buzzing at fifty paces.

"Sorry about my nodding off, (a period of maybe four hours or more.) I think we must wake up the others for a quick pack up and departure from this place. If you go get Bump, I will get Sprig and Luther ready to travel."

The two colleagues were up and moving about in a practiced way with Luther wanting something to eat after his long convalescence. We found some dried fruit and jerky that satisfied us all for now. Monty was busy scattering all the remnants of our camp. The sadness of Sprig seeing her cozy hovel laid bare and melded back into the jungle vegetation was not a pleasant sight for a lovely person. We packed up and left our camp as we had come, in a hurry. Monty led the way through a thick entanglement of bush using Luther's machete. The sounds of men in a sort of frenzy seemed closer than we wanted and were heading in our direction.

CHAPTER NINE

THE TREK UP river in the jungle was like other days with the exception of Luther eventually riding Bump. My buddy wore down about midmorning to the discouragement of the rest of us. Luther was a good sparkplug of encouragement when feeling good. Monty took up the chatter when Luther was ensconced up on Bump. Monty's chatter was not fluid English so that he was in and out his own language and ours. It was almost comical as his English chatter gave off the impression that the jungle was regaling its author with noises of annoyance but when he chanted in his own tongue, the forest quieted with pleasing sounds.

The frenzied sounds of men had died away so that we were sure we had left that disturbance far behind. We made good time during the morning hours even with Luther not feeling so great. The morning being cool and we being refreshed when noontime came. I had estimated we had traveled about four miles. Not too bad, considering the difficulty with the thick vegetation and Bump's huge bulk not liking the snapping branches and occasional sticking of briars. Luther was by now hanging on with only his reserved strength. The heat was sapping what strength we had started with right out of us all. Sprig decided we must halt for a noontime rest. This was met with agreement all round. Even Monty was glad to make the rest stop for his arms must be tired from swinging that machete. A big job for a young Lad.

When we had distributed what little food we had to each person, I suggested to Monty to take the mule close to the river where grass and water would be more plentiful. While in this rested mode, I called Monty to come sit next to me when he returned from his chore of establishing Bump down by the river. I had concluded to show the map to Monty for his evaluation. As Monty sat by me, I very casually pulled out the map and lay it before my young companion. He just as casually glanced at it with amused eyes. "You buy this from old grandpa at tribal jungle bar? Gramps sell many when in young days. Now he old. Sell few maps anymore. This one IS different. Skin much old like Grandpa. Let me look on it a while."

This was good news to my ears. Monty continued to look at the ancient sheepskin map with penetrating inquisitive eyes, complete with a few humming sounds. All of this gave me new hope that my purchase was not a fluke. I put my head close to Monty's expecting some sort of revelation from the engrossed young lad. The only result of this maneuver was that Monty stood up and said: "This is the work of Grandpa and it does look like he has marked an X at a very special place. I have been to this place I think. I know of no good thing there. Grandpa had special powers to know things. My last thinking of him is, he is now dead. The drums have spoken; he has passed over."

Monty handed over the map with some kind of ceremonial gesture that gave me the impression that Monty revered Grandpa. Without another word, he separated himself from me by walking towards Sprig. This news must be shared with Lunch Box while still fresh in my mind.

Luther was on the ground resting and enjoying his time convalescing. He called to me to come and join him. I went over with the old map in my hand, ready to again show it to Luther as I related what Monty had told me just now. Luther was the first to speak.

"Well, old sock what is so important that you look like a cookie snatcher caught in the act. I saw you with Monty each laying on the gibberish and showing him that old fraudulent map"

"Monty seemed to know a lot about this map and its author. He reports it was drawn and sold to me by one of his grandpas. Monty gave me the impression the map could be genuine as it was the last map he sold to a stranger. Monty also said he knew where the X was located. I had hopes when we get to the mission we might engage Monty to guide us to the area where he says the X is located. His only other comment was that no good thing existed at that exact spot, which was nothing but a hill. What do you think?"

"You know me. I will be ready for any old wild goose chase as soon as I get back my strength, and on my pins, which is going to be tomorrow, I am sure. What's to eat?"

Sprig and Monty came over to us with some food that was much appreciated. They reported that Bump was well cared for and that we should soon load up and keep moving after our noon repast. We were certainly in agreement. After a very short noon break, we packed up and began our journey up river. Bump was eager to go because Luther had decided to amble along on foot by holding Bumps tail for assistance. The trail before us began to become more noticeable by being wider and appearing well traveled. Monty kept up chatter about being careful and looking for miner boys. A group he characterized by making the universal sign of a finger pointing to his temple in a rotating gesture. He couldn't or wouldn't elaborate on his gesticulation. We would soon enough find out.

It was Bump, our faithful mule that first gave signs of disturbances. He shot his ears forward and slowed down his advancement. It was all so sudden we barely had time to interpret which was too late. The trail ahead of us began to swell with living human bodies that posed a threatening menace with shouts and gestures no one could misinterpret.

We finally found the miner boys and their vitriolic escapades.

CHAPTER TEN

THE MINER BOYS surrounded us with severe shouting and menacing gestures. Sprig began to converse with what appeared as their leaders. When they came closer, it was quite apparent they were demanding the money owed them. Sprig also told us that the drums had informed them of our approaching this area. She was also informed that three young men of the Chachulu tribe want the map stolen from them back at the southern Jungle Bar. In very short order, Luther was forced to locate the money that Bump was carrying and to turn it over to the young miners that looked like leaders. Luther was constantly voicing his advice that all the miners should get their fair share of the payroll. At this point, it could only be hoped that all would benefit by our retrieving this money. Sprig spent a lot of time and energy getting this truth to the miner boys in charge. The three young natives came out of the jungle and came close to me with sneers and vocal aspersions.

"They want their map back," said a big burly miner of the nefarious kind. I tried to explain I had purchased the map from an old man at the bar fair and square. The three young natives came closer and with newfound boldness, they tried to search my bag and clothes. With much pulling and shoving, the three were convinced I did not have possession of the map at this time. They then moved to Luther with the same song and dance looking for the map. The three cursed and vilified Luther to the point that he began to man handle one of the boys making the young man cry with pain. With this confrontation, the entire gathered group turned their attention to the disturbance, leaving Sprig and Bump free to move about. Sprig handed me the saddlebag where I had secreted the map among our camp supplies. When his two cohorts untangled Luther and the native boy and with some help of a few miner boys, they began a search of Bump's saddlebags, still looking for the map.

When all of the searching produced no results the big miner demanded where the map had been hidden. I tied to convince them that the map was worthless. We treated it as of little or no value so that it would not be found on us. (This was after Sprig had replaced it under Bump's saddle.)"But where is it now," said a small miner in the back? "I saw a small boy run into the jungle just as we met with this group. I'll bet he has it and ran away with the map to thwart the efforts of our three native friends."Monty had retreated into the bush before anyone could have stopped him. The boy moved with lightening like speed, knowing nothing good would befall us or him at the hands of these disgruntled miners and some natives of the sinister kind his people avoided at all costs.

After a period of conjectures and angry finger pointing at Luther, Sprig and I, it appeared that the opposition group of disgruntled persons slowly melted away, taking money and a small amount of medicine bottles with them. Only the three natives remained in the area with the intent of binding us after our capture. You could tell they were not finished with us by a long shot. Without our weapons and in a position of vulnerability the three miscreants with spears pointed made a slipshod affair of binding our hands and tethering our legs to restrict our movements while making another search for the map.

This kind of humiliation was not lessened by the fact the three still had their quivers filled with amateurish constructive arrows. The three boneheads made a mess of all of our remaining supplies and gear without any apparent success. Luther and I remained quiet throughout this ordeal but Sprig made a running commentary aimed at the fruitless efforts of the three young men. She was not bound as completely as Luther and me so that when one of our adversaries struck Bump, Sprig was able to throw a body slam at the offending mess maker. This gave me the chance to free my bonds and attack the Bump batterer. At the same instant, Luther made a valiant lunge at one of the other boys knocking him to the ground. In doing so, the bonds of Luther came undone so that he could pin the boy to the ground. The third bad boy saw his advantage of disappearing so he made a silent exit into the underbrush, post haste. Sprig's fallen villain scrambled to his feet and duplicated his friends' withdrawal into the bush. The last boy stood his ground after Luther permitted him to rise up after Luther's considerable weight was removed. The malefactor jabbered like a machine gun albeit moving slowly backwards to the relative safety of the dense vegetation, where his colleges had disappeared. In a moment, the entire area was fused with a quiet and a sense of earned peace.

The only thing left to do was to clean up the site and hope that the few miles ahead would hold no more terrors that this jungle seemed to serve up any searchers like us.Sprig brought Bump back to the scene of terror where we had narrowly avoided disaster. Bump was unharmed and very calm. We noticed that holding onto his tail for help and façade was one smiling Monty, still in tact and ready to help. When the four of us were reunited, we made short work of cleaning up the mess and packing what few items were left onto the ever-pliant Bump. Before heading out, we discussed the possibility of traveling off this trail to avoid any more confrontations.

"Down by the river we have a lot of undergrowth and roots to contend with and few people travel that way leaving only a faint trail," said Sprig as she looked to Monty for some confirmation. Monty nodded his head in agreement so it was unanimously agreed to try the river route. Hacking our way back down to the river proved to be more strenuous than first believed. Finally approaching the river, we were met with the most loudly of noises imaginable.

CHAPTER ELEVEN

T HE SOUNDS OF the great river horses filled the air with challenges and warnings. The hippotamuses were not directing the bellowing toward us but to several groups wanting the same expanse of water. We carefully avoided the confrontations of bull hippos. On this trail as before, Monty led the way with swinging arcs of Luther's hunting machete that the miner boys and the three youthful adversaries had overlooked.

Sprig began to relate to us that the region looked very familiar and we would be at the mission before nightfall if nothing else unexpected happened. When we took a break Luther took over the clearing the trail to give Monty a respite. The young boy gravitated back to me when we resumed our progress up stream.

Monty spoke to me in a slow, measured, broken English.

"Grandpa says to me miners not have all the good stuff. He say one day he bring best of best to our people before he die. I think maybe we find best of best where map has big X. What you think?"

Knowing this boy for only a short time, I was convinced he was on to something that would provide us with a real adventure and quest. I wondered if Sprig would consent to go with us or remain at her mission with Randall, whoever he was. I still was smitten by this young lady and would make her mine, one way, or another, If Randall were a suitor of Sprig; I would have to be expeditious with my courting of this fair flower in the midst of this uncharted wilderness.

Turning to the boy I said: Are you still wanting to guide me to the area with the X?"

"I be happy to guide you and Mr. Locke to the place marked X on your map. It is a place hard to get to. My Grandpa took me there many years ago. It was a place full of hostile natives and many wild and voracious beasts. We stayed a little while. Grandpa looked all around, shook head, and mumbled to himself, and then we left."

Monty's description gave no clue as to what the X on the map might mean so it could very well be a wild goose chase, as Luther so aptly put, earlier. I knew we would be at great risk without the insight and knowledge of this young native lad.

Moving slowly over to Sprig and Luther, I told them of the plans that I made with Monty. I explained to Sprig that I would love her to go with us, as she knew some of the languages of the regional peoples.

Her response was one of a tepid 'perhaps,' to my mild annoyance. How could I get to know her better if she stayed at the mission while Luther, Monty, and I had all the fun and excitement? She was full of confidence and a sense of humor with many attributes too numerous to mention. Was it a waste on the mission with Pops and Randall? They would be making all the righteous moves, to convince Sprig to stay and not go, I guess. It would be very difficult to explain the reasoning concerning traveling to X when none of us really knew what X might be. Maybe I could convince the mission staff that if Sprig came on along on this journey she could familiarize herself about an area that needed medical help in the future.

When the break was over, I called for us to advance on the mission compound that would soon be in sight, I hoped. Bump was eager to move on, sensing familiar territory. Sprig also moved with a sprightly step that indicated her eagerness to return to familiar surroundings. The day was turning hot as clouds formed to bring their afternoon rain to the awaiting land. No preparations were made for any shelter during this afternoon rain. We just all plodded on and tried to enjoy the coolness of the rain. Soaked to the bone, Sprig announced that we had less that a mile to go.I began to wonder about all of the skirmishes and discontent in the area and if it might be smart to enter the compound with a great deal of caution. When I related this concern to Luther and Sprig they were quick to agree. We told Monty to begin to advance quietly after we told him of our concern. This we all did until we saw the buildings before us. At this point, we agreed by motions, that only one-person go forward to investigate the compound for friendly or foe, greeters. I accepted the challenge without any dissent. Moving forward with as much skill that I could muster, I saw the buildings that appeared to be abandoned.A fence surrounded the compound that had many gaps in its construction so I could view most of the grounds without entering. Still not wanting to stand up or motion the others to follow I just waited. Eventually I gave out an anemic, "hello the mission." No response was my reply. This quiet answer was enough for me to stand up and shout with some vigor and determination. "Any body in the mission compound? I am a friend and need some assistance before entering the mission grounds." If anyone is listening that last comment may bring him or her to the surface.

Upon close visual scrutiny, I saw a body moving about the grounds. It was a small body moving quickly to and fro. I was surprised to finally realize it was Monty inside the fence. That young one had entered the compound without detection and reconnoitered the area to the extent he waved us all in with the comment, "No one here." When we all gathered inside the fenced area Sprig began to go from building to building calling out her dad's name for some kind of hopeful response. Sadly, Monty's statement that 'no one here' held true. Sprig was beside herself with grief as hot tears began to overflow her beautiful azure blue eyes. When I went to comfort her I was met with the most enjoyable embrace imaginable. She only emoted for a short time before beginning to plan a strategy for determining what has happened to her colleagues. She had earlier told me that the mission also employed two local women and one man besides her dad and Randall. A total of five persons to account for.

She began with an aura of inbred authority. "We must break into two groups to search out the buildings for any clues to what has happened here. I will take Bump back to the barn area and will gather with the group back here in a few minutes. While I am gone if anyone thinks of anything to make this exercise more efficient, just divulge it upon my return. With a smile that would melt steel she turned to gather Bump and return him to his barn.

Luther and I became speechless as Sprig moved away as the wood nymph she most represented. Monty was first to break the silence. "I see blood trail at big house. Not much only little. Mr. Straight and I should go there first so we not frighten lady." The little man was again right on target, so we told Luther were Monty and I would start so he could tell Sprig where we were.

The two us moved to the big house that most probably was the living quarters for the Gardeners and Randall. The blood trail was slight as we followed it to a small out building behind the big house. Monty in his boyish enthusiasm and confidence yanked opened the door exposing a body on the floor. The body was trussed up and gagged. As I bent low to determine if this victim was alive I was relieved to find the old boy still among the living even though unconscious. Monty and I started for the big house, most probably the living quarters for Gardeners and Randall. Monty showed me the blood rail and it was slight just as he had said earlier.

CHAPTER TWELVE

THE OLD BODY on the floor was curled up in a fetal position. A small trickle of blood had dried on his intelligent forehead. His white hair had fallen onto a blood smear and matted tight to his skin as the blood dried. Pulling the gag, I began to gently untie his bonds. His attackers used some old lamp wire and the knots offered up a challenge to untie. When the man was completely free of all his physical restraints, Monty threw some water on the face of the one time prisoner. This gesture revived the old fellow, no doubt Sprig's father. With some sputtering and gasping for breath, the old gentlemen came around shortly being revived.

Monty left the small shed to report to the other persons in our team. In short order, Sprig and Luther were crowding into the confined space. Sprig was able to squeeze by me to minister to her father. Even though this was a pleasant maneuver, I knew enough to move back outside as a very determined daughter nursed Mr. Gardener back to life.

While I was outside I pulled at Luther to get a report on the other buildings in the compound.

"Every building has been trashed and looted. We found no other persons dead or alive in any of the buildings we searched. It looks like a vindictive attack of constrained proportions. No burnings or general mayhem or wanton destruction. It appears like a message was meant instead of wholesale destruction. The folks around about still want the benefits of the mission but wanted to vent their anger at anyone that might represent Caucasian authority."

"A pretty good assessment, old stick. Let's wait until Sprig's father can shed more light on the subject, before we make plans."

Looking into the shed I was pleased that Sprig had brought the old boy back to the present and was questioning dad about the mission's disorder as well as his wounded condition. His voice was weak but I could hear his tale of woe as Sprig made the effort to comfort him as he revealed his story of peril and shock. When Mr. Gardener calmed down and apparently ran out of steam, Sprig had us take him back to his house and put him to bed. The big house did not suffer as much devastation as the other buildings. Was this a sign of the respect for the mission head or had the hooligans just ran out of steam when coming to the big house?

When Mr. Gardener was properly settled in bed and resting, Sprig began to pour out the details of her conversation with her dad.

"Dad said that the miner boys came in with some local troublemakers trying to locate their pay from the mine. When dad told them of the unexpected delay they didn't believe him. They began a haphazard search of the premises starting with his house. When they found no money, they began searching the other buildings. Each search became more violent than the previous. All the while Randall Potts, dad's assistant, kept up with the searchers while voicing threats and cajoling them to quit. This made the local toughs mad. They eventually hit Randall to render him unconscious. At this time, they came back to dad and when they got negative answers from him, they clobbered him and trussed him up while putting him in the shed for safe keeping. Dad said they took the old boy into the woods and that was the last time he saw Randall. All of our local helpers had long since departed the compound for a safer location. When I told him about the plane crash he indicated his thinking, was along these lines so he had by radio asked for a duplicate or repeat order? He was told that it would be very difficult for monies and drugs to be sent right away, indicating a delay of several days. He was waiting for the replacing order when all this happened."

"What can we do now, Sprig, to help you and your dad."

I spilled that offer so fast I didn't even have time to think the comment through. Sprig seemed so vulnerable at this point; my concern for her situation became the most important thing for me to address.All this time Monty and Luther were investigating the entire area for any clues to determine all that happened here. When this task was completed, I saw the two head out of the fenced area into the dense vegetation surrounding the mission. With a few hoots and hollers, the two shouted back that they had found the assistant tied to a tree and still alive. Randall Potts was brought back to the big house where he was revived back to his senses. Randal was about fifty with a slightly balding head and protruding eyes of the owlish type. His broken glasses hung crazily down still affixed to a swollen fighters ear. He was skinny as a rail as though he didn't get to the supper table on time. His thin lips quivered slightly as he spoke. He repeated the scene that Mr. Gardener had made known to us, previously. His head was sporting a nice sized lump where the hoodlums had anesthetized him. He also had a plethora of bruises and cuts to his credit. Randall was sent off to bed after Sprig's kindly nursing ministrations.

Sprig answered my question and told us we were free to leave or we could stay here at the mission for few days. I was ready to offer our help in putting the place back in shape but I knew I couldn't speak for Luther or Monty.

Luther was first to voice an opinion on the subject: "Well old bean what do we do now? Should we stick around here and help in the clean up or take off on our search for X?" "I think we must stay and help here until some normalcy returns. This also would go a long was in enticing Sprig to accompany us on our trek towards X. I don't know how long it will take but we can play it by ear if that meets with your approval."

"Dix you know me better than that. I will stay and help. At this juncture in my life, this is the best of all possibilities; especially here, in the jungle watching you court the fair lady. If you stumble I'll be here to catch you."

We stayed about two weeks as all was put back in order with Randall and the local helpers back in the yoke of service and confident existence. Even Monty stayed, saying it was the most fun he had had in many a moon. Money was paid to the miners with the proviso that some funds would revert to Mr. Gardener and his mission for repairs etc. All was in place to ask Sprig if she would make the trek with us to find the import of X if any existed. I finally got up the courage to ask her to join us since her Dad and the mission was back in working order. I was slightly encouraged by the days spent with her that proved to have some bonding results, since I continued to court her with her Dad's hesitant permission. Sprig was hanging up wash when I approached her. "Sprig, have you thought anymore about going with us on our journey to X?" I held my breath for the coming answer.

CHAPTER THIRTEEN

S PRIG WAS NOT surprised at my question. She looked at me with her piercing blue eyes and spoke with a confidence that indicated she had thought about this possibility for some time.

"I took my dad into my confidence about traveling with you on your expedition to the place of X on your map. I was surprised when he voiced a kind evaluation of you and Luther. He told me you had shown him the map and he was intrigued by it and your resolve to pursue the journey as part of every boy's dream. Dad was also impressed concerning you and Luther's talents and dedication putting the mission back in operational status. With all this in mind he gave me permission to decide for myself about the expedition, if Monty acts as chaperon."

It sounded to me as a qualified yes that I could live with. Sprig was giving me a no nonsense smile that spoke volumes to me.

"This qualification comes to me with a ready and hearty yes. Monty has indicated his desire to go with us and guide us to the place his old granddaddy took him when he was just a wee lad. When will you be ready so we can start soon?"

"Not so fast, oh eager one. It will take a few more days for me to put together the things required for such a journey. I want to make an exhaustive journal awhile we travel. Dad will want me to take medical supplies in case we need them. Toothaches can popup at the most inconvenient time. He also suggested we carry some essential tools and baubles if we meet up with some people that like to trade and not to annihilate. All of this will take some time and planning."

"That's all o.k. With me. I am sure Luther will agree."

"I am also wanting to leave Bump here because of several considerations. He was bitten up pretty badly in the jungle. It will take some more time for him to heal. He also is used around the mission for plowing duty and wagon pulling from time to time. That means you boys will have to load your packs to the hilt since this trip appears to be quite some distance from here."

The thought of heavy, cumbersome packs being lugged through the steaming jungle gave me some thoughts of canceling the trek. Knowing Sprig would be close by dissolved those thoughts immediately. After all, what was I made of, steel or smoke? I gave Sprig the thumbs up sign and told her I would tell Luther and Monty what to expect in the coming days. As I left this meeting, I headed for Luther and Monty where they were intensely playing ping pong in one of the larger rooms in the mission complex. When I relayed all that was discussed with Sprig earlier, both expressed satisfaction with all Sprigs' suggestions as well as her timetable for beginning.

Monty was very excited as he told of the joy he felt in going back to a place his granddad took him a few years before. "Grandpa always thought of that place with a certain reverence," said Monty.

What really piqued my curiosity was the fact that Monty saw the X as a real place. Monty had mentioned that his Grandpa was a sort of spirit that liked to play tricks on people, especially strangers from the American continent. He had sold many nostrums, maps, and instruments of magic to unsuspecting strangers. Monty saved me from my humiliation by stating that the old sheep skin map he owned, he never sold. "This map was always carried by grandpa but never sold until he came to you in his last days. He knew some how you were going to the mission and Ms. Sprig." Great comfort to me from the mouth of a babe.

The next two days flew by with a rapidity that numbed the senses. Monty was supplied with a daypack so that his load was not too rigorous for the young boy. He said he needed fewer things because what ever he required he could get from the jungle's abundance. Herb gardener saw fit to advance us with a rifle and revolver with the admonition that nothing adverse should befall his only daughter. The other things that Lunch Box and I packed away included, dry food, light clothing, including bee keepers netted hats. Slickers to ward off the rains, heavy boots, and one blanket each with Monty carrying a spare. Cooking utensils plus a few assorted items Sprig imposed our way with pleading eyes, fairly well completed our packing. The packs were quite heavy. Luther reminded us that after a few gastronomical delights the weight would decrease. This only eased our thinking not our burdensome packs. I could see that his pack bulged to the extent that caused me to know his pack was heaviest of all. Ample supplies of tasty food no doubt. We all agreed to set out in the morning at sunrise.

It was difficult to sleep this night because of all the adrenalin surging through me. I could hear Luther sawing logs in the bunk next to mine. Monty slept on the floor with his little thin blanket for comfort and familiarity. He didn't want to get too comfortable sleeping on the bunks thin mattresses. My mind wandered over the last few weeks trying to digest all of the events which my mental faculties could hardly take it all in. The search for the plane had netted us only a few remnants of its contents. We returned what we could to Mr. Gardener and helped in the cleanup of the trashed compound. We had not fully determined the fate of the pilot. My heart had been stolen by Sprig and was still in her possession. She had consented to accompany Luther, Monty, and I on the journey to X. That was a good sign for me. Maybe I am making some headway in the courting department. As sleep began to overtake me, I was surprised that the relationship between Sprig and me had the effect of displacing all of the dangers and pitfalls that might lie ahead. I fell asleep with a sense that I had resolved all of the difficult pending issues.

CHAPTER FOURTEEN

I WAS LATE IN rising having overslept because of sweet dreams. The compound sounded busy and productive. As I was dressing, Luther stuck his head into the room and shot me one of his caustic remarks. "Well, old bud, it is nice to see you up before the sun sets. We have been hard at work packing all of the gear for the trip into the interior. I hope you can throw some things together so we can begin before nightfall."

"Why didn't you call me, earlier?"

"I thought you needed the rest since you will carry the heaviest pack while leading the way. It was also nice to not have you nagging and directing all of the activity for once. When you are ready come on outside and review all of the packing to be up to your standards."

As I walked outside, Sprig was there will a cup of hot coffee and a slice of jellied bread she had fixed for me. I thought this gesture was an indication of me finally penetrating the cool shell of this girl. Maybe not! As I was handed the cup she remarked: "We have done most of the work in packing but your final acceptance must be necessary to go forth."

"Is Monty around and packed also?"

"Yes he was first up to start early this morning."

"I guess as I fill my own pack could one of you make a list so that I could see what is ready to go and if we are missing anything."

"I've already prepared a list, oh great one. Cast your eyes on the completeness and variety of articles we have assembled," offered Lunch Box

"I see that Monty is not on the list."

"He personally assured me that all he needed was his blanket, machete, knife, a line complete with hook and a few odds and ends. I felt he knew more about interior travel then you and I, so I just let it be."

Sprig began to justify her pack's contents, which I thought unnecessary and gently assured her that all was quite adequate, even though books and toiletries were low on my list of necessary items to tote for a long distance.

"Luther, if you will help me get my things together maybe Sprig can say her good byes to Herb and Randall as well as rounding up Monty for our departure."

I was pleased to see each of my friends moved to my directives, cheerfully.

I finished packing as Sprig and her father along with Randal came over to wish us a safe trip and admonishments to be safe. Herb also made it a point especially to me that Sprig should be protected at all times with further urgings to not let her take unnecessary chances. All of this required time and emotions that included hugs and tears. We finally hefted our packs with Monty coming over to lead the procession into the great jungle with its foreboding under brush. Sprig continued to look back to the consternation of Luther, into which she bumped several times.Monty was happy as he led us down the unfamiliar trail we had not used previously.

He seemed to know where he was going, even though the map showed our destination many miles from this location. Monty's certain swings of his machete from time to time, stirred up the waiting myriad of unpleasant insects. This time we all brought beekeepers hats complete with netting down to our shoulders. Monty laughed at the chapeau with some mockery in his eyes. His only comment was by way of actively giving Sprig a fan made of the of some bracken he had picked earlier. With a demonstration of waving it in front of him, he inferred this is what the natives do. We soon saw the advantage of this simple solution to a perplexing problem when our beekeepers hats began to be ripped and torn to the many snags from the branches overhanging the trail. Monty very graciously made fans for all of us as we saw the benefits of this simple device. It was a life changing moment for the young lad. From this day, forward we treated him more like an adult and he realized it.

The morning seemed to just melt away as the group became melted into a cohesive unit on a highly mysterious trek. We talked a great deal and revealed some our most interesting traits as adventurers and developing human beings. Lunch Box was the most vocal to spread out his past life and his hopes for the future.

"I have always wanted to taste the unknown and to participate in some adventures. My Past has been filled with education and adhering to parental directives. I would like to help my fellowman and please my God with beneficial activity. Later I want to marry and raise a family. I sense a calling to be a good husband and father so that the world will be a better place when I leave than when I came into.

Sprig was mildly shocked to hear this friend reveal so much without any regrets or hesitancy. I knew Luther had periods of thoughtfulness in this realm of domesticity and expressions of reverence. Luther continued until he felt the need for someone else to disclose their innermost thoughts of the future. Just as I was ready to take up the torch Monty emitted a shout to stop.

"I see smoke on top of trees far a way. I must go to see if good smoke or bad smoke." Without another word, the boy slipped off down the trail like sand from a bottle.

After Monty left so quick, the three of us formed a little cluster to talk about this little disturbance in our forward trek.

"I thought I smelled wood smoke a moment ago," said Luther with a quizzical look that was entirely foreign to Mr. Luther Locke. "Monty has eyes and a snuffer that beats mine."

Sprig was still puzzled, "I don't see smoke or smell it. Oh! Now I do."

It was no time when all of us could see and smell the smoke rising over the top of trees a fair distance off.

Luther was the first to offer some kind of explanation. "It is most probably a bonfire to celebrate some great feat or celebration."

Sprig not to be out done said in her most authoritative voice with overtones of good humor: "It more likely a fire to begin a war party or to cook some unfortunate victim." We spent some more time speculating about the smoke. It brought back to my mind that old saying. 'Where there is smoke there is fire.' Monty returned with a look of anxiety on his little smooth brow. "I am thinking it is a bad fire." This was going to be a great adventure, I was certain.

CHAPTER FIFTEEN

MONTY TRIED TO tell us with his halting English that the smoke ahead was a great forest fire, engulfing brush and tree alike. "The wind is pushing the fire to us. We will have to hike back over to the river and cross it to keep a way from the hot flames. Without further adieu, we all turned and headed for the river, now about two or three miles away. The trail was faint until we came to a place that was torn all to pieces by warthogs. We carefully approached the damaged area not certain if the perpetrators were still on the scene. Keeping our weapons at the ready we were pleased the place was no longer occupied by the culprits. That action saved our bacon, because charging out of the surrounding bush came three vicious baboons. With frightening speed, they charged us with menacing gestures and threatening sounds. We discharged our weapons close to the three to cause them to cease and desist. This result was made more complete by the quick response by Monty. In the wink of an eye, he had his sling shot out, utilizing it as a very viable weapon. This caused one of the baboons' considerable pain by a broadside, bulls eye on the bigger of the brutes. Behind us came an even bigger male with destruction in his attack. He uncharacteristically came with little warning. For some reason he headed for little Monty, maybe because he was the smallest target. Without thinking or mental debating, I pulled out my revolver and shot the beast right behind his eyes. He stopped in his murderous flight and fell to the ground with only a little twitching until the last gasp of savage life left his crumpled body. It was a scary thing to witness, as I was one not too keen on killing wild animals, unnecessarily. My fear was that Sprig would think less of me because of rashness. Looking towards her, I saw no condemnation in her gaze in my direction. We were all stunned but not paralyzed. When all was once again quiet, we agreed that danger could come in more than one form. This made us all more alert and primed for the unexpected. This was not going to be a walk in the park.

Continuing down the trail, I knew we would have to stop again for a noon rest and lunch. Thinking back to the packing up we had brought only some meager supplies of food that would be quick to prepare and eat. Monty assured us more than once he could supply us with meat when it became necessary. With that in mind, Luther had packed many herbs and spices to enliven any common food to heights of culinary excellence. With these thoughts on my mind, I approached Monty with the question, "what will you get for our supper tonight?" Monty answered with a twinkle in his eyes, "Mr. Lunch Box beat you to the punch about that. He already has asked that some fat ground birds to be roasted slowly roasted over a fire. I will do my best to trap some jungle chickens for supper. I was sure that we thought of other things but food was important.

Looking over at Sprig, she was glistening with perspiration. Her clothes, like Luther's, looked so soaked it was drawing many flying insects looking for a tasty salty treat and in so doing we all used our fans with a kind of frantic butterfly burlesque parody. Only Monty appeared to be content under the blazing sun and humid trail. Taking out my compass and making notes caused us to stop more frequently than I liked. The Old map came out about every few hours to give me confirmation that what we were doing had a spark of intelligence mixed with anticipation. Seeing the river come into view was an encouragement. We knew to cross at this point was too dangerous as Monty pointer out the markings of crocodiles. We would have to find a very shallow ford to cross with safety.

Luther came out with a possible concern. "Do you think the fire would jump the river and eventually meet us on the other side?"

Monty gave the answer by using a type of proverb, "you can make plans in the day, but in the night anything is possible."

Luther had to have that explained to him by Sprig: "Anything could happen regardless of our well thought out plans. The answer to your question earlier is maybe."

We followed the river until we came to a shallow place we could ford without the danger of crocodiles. Wading into the water it wasn't long before we realized that near the rivers center the depth caused us the sink down until our packs were in danger of being drenched. Little Monty was already carrying his pack on top of his head as he made the crossing look easy when he walked out on the other side refreshed and pack dried. He looked at all of us in a queer sort of way wondering why we didn't follow his lead.

"Well, that was refreshing, I see that sprig wants to inspect her pack for any water seepage since she is shorter that us," said Luther with wisp of guilt in his voice for not offering to help the young lady. I felt the same. We both approached Sprig with apologies spoken in awkward whispers.

Sprig was evidently surprised as she responded by informing us that she could take care of herself: Quit fussing over me boys. I am able to fend for myself. Don't try to baby me or I will turn into some kind of city girl you would not appreciate." With that mild but insightful rebuke, we left Sprig to rummage in her pack for anything that might be wet. Monty knelt down beside her and offered his help in a childlike way as Luther and I ambled over to some shade by a tree to watch the progress of our friends. A few pieces of clothing were pulled out into the sunshine by Sprig who had Monty spread them onto a waiting bush for drying. "They will dry in no time," she said to no one in particular. Of course, she was right. We took the time to rest and break out some packed quick food for hurried consumption. We all looked at the map again hoping for some sign we might have missed before. Compass headings were recorded in my little book as I noticed Sprig also writing in her journal.

CHAPTER SIXTEEN

THE REST WAS most invigorated causing all of us to step out along the river with renewed strength and anticipation. The map showed we would have to recross the river eventually. This caused us some concern because we were headed towards the area where smoke could still be seen. This possible complication did not deter us in our advance or pace.

With Monty still in the lead, it was disquieting to see him coming back through the line to whisper in my ear. "With fire still up ahead it will cause all kinds of animals to move in our direction. Not only grazing animals but many of the big tooth creatures and giants of the jungle that might not hesitate to harm us."

"It might be best if we began to circle around this area to avoid any animal confrontations."

Monty shook his head like he understood everything I had just said. Moving up the line, he informed all to follow his new direction. When once again in the lead he made a ninety-degree turn into the bush after finding the faintest of game trails. Small creatures made this trail so we had to stoop and dodge a lot of brush making the going slow and uncomfortable. Just as we were making better time and becoming acclimated to the brush difficulties, the darkening clouds of afternoon rains reminded us. The drops came with a ferocity not experienced before. The torrent came with large droplets hitting our bodies with stinging, slapping violence causing all of us to seek some kind of shelter to wait out this present unexpected conundrum. We followed Monty as he headed for an area of trees that were thick and inviting. Stripping bark off a certain tree of great size, using our machetes, we soon had a roof to cover our bodies. Sitting down on the smallest of spaces that was sandy, Monty quickly had saplings and branches to support our bark coverings. In only minutes, we were all enclosed in a viable shelter to wait out this storm. The wind tugged at the sides of our shelter with no apparent damage. Noises of all kind accompanied the deluge.

I was the first to speak: "This torrent should put out the fire in the forest giving an opportunity to get back on the other side of this river."

"This is true but remember that the water will certainly rise in the river, causing us a real challenge to get back across. It also would be nice to find a place that is dry for our evening camp." Sprig was not worried about her pack getting wet because she had make certain that it was packed in such a way to minimize any water seepage after her river crossing.

The wind and rain seemed to go on for hours but towards late afternoon the deluge suddenly stopped as it had started. While we waited, it was decided that this place was as good as any to make camp. Not as dry, as Sprig might want but no animals had been detected of any size or hostile beings of any kind for that matter.

We gathered dead wood hanging from the branches to begin a cook fire. The dense vegetation should dissipate any tell tale smoke to keep us safe from any indigenous people that might resent our presence. Luther prepared to assemble a fine meal as Sprig wrote in her journal. Monty was busy constructing several hammocks out of local vegetation, using only his knife and machete. By the time the sun was beginning to dip in the west and leave us, we had formed a tidy bona fide camp. Cozy, mostly dry and conducive to sleep for the next day's challenges.

With Sprig and Monty in their hammocks and Luther and I in our tent we were not even disturbed by occasional nighttime stirrings of animals and critters. The sounds by now were accepted and routine to the extent they added to the rhythms that helped sleep.

The morning came as harmonious as the evening went. Birds sang their songs of greeting with whistles and screeching too mysterious to label them disturbing. Critters moved through the underbrush avoiding direct contact with the human interlopers, but just barely. Monty was up and had a small cook fire ready for someone to orchestrate a hearty breakfast. The sun was up and causing a slight mist to rise after the torrent of yesterday. I gathered all of the utensils for the morning repast intending to try my hand at breakfast vittles. Before I knew it, Sprig was beside me with her gentle and smooth body gently moving me out of her way. I had detected in days past this was her way of taking on a task she liked. For me the gesture reeked of compatibility of our work responsibilities.Luther was coming out of our tent like an old bear exiting his hibernation den. Luther headed for the coffee I had made earlier, with sleep still in his eyes. With a few hot swigs, he was ready for the day ahead. His loud and merry comments were heard by all and for a hundred yards around. "Well, what is on the agenda for today? I think I can hike all day without a complaint."

He might not be so happy if he knew what interesting things lay ahead. The storm had abated last night so that no uninvited quests came into camp. We finished our morning meal that Sprig has so lovingly prepared. She was writing in here journal when I called for a pack up and get out for the crew. "We need to make up some lost time for the several hours we had made this snug camp." The crew responded without complaints or hesitations of my command.

Monty was busy taking down the hammocks and destroying them to making it difficult for anyone to come onto this spot and know we were here. He put out and covered the fire as expert as anyone I had ever seen. The little thatched shelter was also torn down and scattered throughout the thick jungle. Monty was certainly the most valuable of guides and an affable companion.

CHAPTER SEVENTEEN

W HEN ALL WAS in readiness we packed up all of our belongings, exiting the area by the way we came in. Monty was busy brushing out our last remaining footprints by a branch and walking backwards. I always felt Monty knew more than us by his constant vigilant behavior. The young lad moved to the front passing a surprised and annoyed Luther, who had desired to lead for a while. Monty had confided in me earlier that he should lead again this morning for a short distance to the river. I had accepted his recommendation without question, giving him permission to lead for a time, without telling Luther. Not wanting any of our team to be vexed, I slipped by Sprig with a comment. "I need to talk to Luther a minute."

Sprig, with her all knowing smile answered in whisper. "I think you should before a rubbing becomes a blister."

Finding Luther in a slightly pouty mood, I explained my decision. "Monty is uncertain about the dangers in this region and he convinced me to send him on in the lead to sniff out any unexpected dangers of this jungle. Luther was very relieved to hear this. "So I am not relieved of my duty to lead some of the time?"

"Of Course not. We need Monty to use all his skills when we travel in such close quarters in these uncharted waters."

"By the way Dix is the map showing any visible landmarks in the journey we take today?"

"The next landmark after crossing this river is a swampy region we might advance to today. The map shows a large area with water, tress, stumps, and a narrow pathway through the maze. I am of the opinion that we can get through it if we stay on the narrow serpentine path. I am hopping Monty has been there so we can avoid any quicksand or quagmires."

"Lead on oh splendid one. I am as happy as a lark."

As Luther moved up the line to settle in behind Monty's expertly wielded machete, Sprig moved up close to me. In this very small trail, it was impossible to travel two abreast. She wanted know what the entire hubbub was about between Luther and myself.

"Luther was interested in Monty leading this morning and what new signs the map showed for this part of the trek."

"Well, what are they?"

I related all that Luther and I had talked about throwing my voice over my shoulder. When Sprig indicated she was satisfied, I had her move ahead of me so that I once again brought up the rear. We were nearing river and could still smell wood smoke but is of the wet and acrid variety. The wind had its way by blowing right into our faces, causing displeased faces to turn away. This turning away was to our advantage because in so doing we spied some indigenous hunters looking for any animals that might have been overcome by fire or smoke. Monty signaled us to drop and freeze, which we did without hesitation. There were four of them. Stooping close to the ground looking for tracks or spoor they were totally engrossed in their quest. Armed with only spears and bows they did not appear as formidable obstacles but a confrontation could give an entire area notice of our objectionable presence. Cramped in a stooped position we held our breath until the four passed our present heading. Slowing rising to a standing position we became more cautious than before since we were now certain some hostiles roamed this area.

Monty signed us to slowly follow him to the riverbank. Here we examined the river to see if crossing would be difficult. We all were chagrined to see how high the water flowed. This presented a new hurdle to overcome. We gathered to gather by a large tree to make new plans and keep from exposing our selves unnecessarily. With little or no choice, we followed the river until it spread out or presented a place that some kind of bridge might be constructed. Someone had opined that the locals must have away to cross even at flood time. With that thought in mind, Luther took the lead along the water way with its faint trail beckoning us forward. Along the river, we again encountered slippery paths, protruding roots and low hanging branches. The insects became problematic as we stirred them up by brushing the vegetation and presenting new warm bodies to attack. We hiked for what seemed like miles before coming to a narrow place, that one could cross by felling trees long enough to carefully pass over to the other side. Just as we made preparations to fell a tree, Sprig's beautiful eyes searched out and found a swinging bridge across the river only a hundred yards farther along.

With great caution, we approached the bridge with apprehension and trepidation, not knowing if the owners were in a position to protect or deny its use.

Quietly I asked Monty to made a reconnaissance of the area and return with a report on the feasibility to cross the river unnoticed. The lad moved off into the brush, silently and disappeared. The rest of us huddled behind a great clump of brush to wait for Monty's return.

"It seems to me we send that boy off on the most dangerous missions when he is not really involved in the out come of this possible fiasco."

"Sprig, if we hit pay dirt of any kind on this expedition, Monty is to share and share alike."

"I concur, oh generous one. We will all be glad to view Monty as an equal partner in all we do or any spoils we find on this search."

"I just worry about the little fellow taking on so much responsibility and danger, being so young."

We were all in agreement, as we waited. The time dragged on until I suggested, I should go after him and see if the boy had encountered any difficulties. As I was removing my backpack, Monty appeared with anxiety on his face. With his tardy reappearance, we could only guess at the cause. We waited with bated breath for the young boy's report and recommendations.

CHAPTER EIGHTEEN

MONTY WAS EXCITED but not flummoxed. His eyes took on a sparkle with golden brown flecks in them that gave him an older and more sophisticated appearance beyond his years.

"I am most honored to spy out the land for you. A great tribe is in the near land. They are most vicious but also smart with works, like the bridge. I stumbled into one of their guard pits that help them protect the village. It took me time to finally scramble out with the help of my knife. The people are not very alert, because one of the village dogs barked at me without any response from people inside their circle. They have vines in the trees with stones attached to help ward of any invaders. The men have shrunken heads on pole outside the huts to show others of great deeds. Each hut has its own fire pit inside the shelter, with smoke coming out the top. Very smart. If we cross the bridge, we must do it when dark because the village can see the bridge from where it stands."

"We are most grateful for your report and will follow your recommendation if we all decide to use the bridge as our means to cross the raging river." I went on with some of my own thoughts.

"What can we do between now and dark? We have about fours hours before the sun goes down. We would have to travel far to make a camp and it would have to be without fire."

Luther was thinking hard by the wrinkled brow and intent eye contact with me when he said: "Why don't we run across the bridge and cut its supporting ropes when we reach the other side?"

Oh sure. We do that and every village within a hundred miles would be informed by the speaking drums of our dastardly deed and tell of the rewards and honor of capturing or killing us."

Sprig was aware of the effectiveness of the speaking drums because she had heard them and her dad had used them on occasion. Monty spoke up and gave a new suggestion that was very intelligent. "We could go way around this village and come back to river to see if any narrow place farther along. There we could try and cut a big tree and cross on our own at a easy pace." "That's a good plan but time wise we would have gain nothing. Our best bet is to stay here and suffer a little without hot coffee or cooked food and tackle the bridge this evening," I said as the faces looking at me turned into frowns and thin lips. Slowly but surely, the huddled group gave nods of assent that warmed my heart. We found a spot about a quarter mile away that had a miniscule clearing were we rested or dozed until the sun began its descent in the west. The afternoon rain did not come this day so the sky was leaden and threatening. Belated rumblings with some flashes of heat lightening gave the sky a menacing pall over the area causing all of us to be slightly uneasy on our return to the bridge. Sprig offered to go first with her petite frame. I was against it but held my peace, as she wanted to demonstrate her willingness to participate in all phases of any dangers. Monty also offered to go first but we had decided he had taken enough chances with dangerous features this day.

Sprig hunched down as she approached the bridge in the early darkness. We could still hear noises from the village with its normal evening activities. Sprig shot across the bridge like it was made of hot coals. Safely across, she disappeared from sight. With that triumph in hand, Monty was sent across next. He made the same fluid crossing that Sprig had made. I asked Luther to go next as he was chomping at the bit to get on the other side. Being the heaviest of the four with the bulkiest pack his crossing had more movement and notice that the others. After he disappeared on the other side, I noticed a young boy come close to the bridge from the village. He looked all around before entering the bridge and began to jump up and down to make it sway and hop. In a short period of time a female came to the boy and with some heated words pulled him off and unceremoniously dragged the youngster back to the village. After a reasonable length of time, I warily moved down to the bridge, feeling like I was on stage with millions watching. On the other side three very concerned travelers that had experienced the same sensation I had, met me. I moved across with no notice of any kind from the villagers. With only hand signals, we began to march out of that area with a certain kind of urgency. Only out stomachs growled as we moved down what looked like a well-worn path away from the dangers behind us. The starlight only gave us only fleeting glances at the trail. Monty led the way with his young eyes close to the ground. After traveling like this for about an hour, Monty turned off the trail trying to find a secluded spot to camp for the night. He finally stopped at a place that was a depression, probably because of the knot of trees to hide our fire and give some protection if hostiles stumbled on us. The only negative that I brought up was the fact if a storm or rain fell on us here we would be inundated with water. Monty assured me, "no rain tonight, will come tomorrow."

We had come to trust the lad so we pitched right in to make our nighttime camp. The hammocks appeared seemingly like magic from the busy fingers of Monty. Luther and I put our tent up, as Sprig was getting ready to cook some food and make some coffee. I gathered some wood to build the fire and in no time, we had ourselves a cozy little functioning campsite.

After supper, I noticed Sprig writing in her journal. I took the opportunity to go over and sit next to her. I was going to wait until she looked up and noticed me but her writing continued unabated. Finally, I spoke up, "We had a lot of interesting things happen today. What one did you find the most interesting?" She looked up from her journal and replied with as much sincerity she could muster, after being interrupted. "Everyday is interesting with you along, Mr. Dickson Straight." I took it as a positive comment and finally engaged the young lady in more conversation.

CHAPTER NINETEEN

SPRIG AND I talked for along time until the others told us to be quiet and go to our bed or hammock. We retired to get prepared to meet our future and to uncover X. Luther in the tent was already snoring. I felt maybe I should stay up longer as we had not assigned guard duty for the night season. I slipped out of the tent and climbed up the slight incline to find a place to sit and listen. Finding a deadfall tree, I sat down and began to ponder our situation. Sprig had said she was not so immersed in the X thing, but she liked the travel and adventure. The trip ahead was even more arduous than what we had come through. Would our luck hold out in this dangerous and forbidding land? Was it right for me to expect a young lad and beautiful lass to travel this region? The map was purchased under spurious conditions. Everyone had viewed it as a hoax. Did Monty really have a sense of honor with us or was he leading us into a situation more deadly than we could imagine? After all his loyalty must lay with his tribe and family. I was certain I could trust Luther with anything as we have had a long and varied relationship. Sprig was another matter. Did she like me or was her attentions manifested for other reasons? What about the constant annoyances of the three amigos? Did they follow us to kill or to try and wrest the map from us for their own spurious reasons?I felt I was slowly becoming paranoid and would have to find some sleep before my thoughts rambled into uncharted waters. As I got up from my sitting position, I heard noises in the undergrowth. Upon close observation, I determined that at least two brown bodies had been spying out our campfire with its dying embers. Waiting for a moment, the two turned into three upon scrutiny. My mind flashed back to the three that have been following us for many days and weeks. I dared not move for fear they would attack the camp or me in our weakened position. After an indeterminate time the three forms moved away from their place of concealment. I was tempted to follow but decided it was best for me to wake Luther and have him take over the sentry duty until he wanted Monty to replace him. Maybe I was so tired I had imagined the recent event. It would be best to alert Luther to the possibilities at any rate.

Moving down the depression's slope I was surprised to see Monty slipping back into his hammock as though he had been awake and on watch as I had been. Waking Luther was not as arduous as I had envisioned, the great bear coming forth from his hibernation. Telling Luther of my suspicions and of the experience on the lip of the depression, I was again surprised, that Luther was in complete agreement to my suspicions.

"I'll keep a weather eye out for any unusual movements. My revolver will be my companion so not to worry. Go get some sleep and I'll wake Monty for the early morning sentry duty if I tire at all." Taking Luther's comments at face value I entered the tent and fell asleep with in moments of hitting my head on the pillow.

In the morning, I awoke with the rising sun and the muted chatter of Monty and Luther around the cook fire. Assuming all was in order, I dressed and presented myself to the two early birds. "Monty has confided with me that he had also felt the presence of others last night. Not seeing any sentry, he felt it would be best if he made the rounds to locate anybody on the prowl. He got up and avoiding you went around the rim of the depression only to find three hostiles keeping an eye on our camp and its fire. Watching for some time they appeared not ready to make any aggressive movements towards us. When they left he returned to his hammock, seeing you making your way down the slope."

"I can't figure why these three are making such a long enterprise to thwart our efforts to get to the place marked X. You would think they are on a quest of serious proportions."

"I think they want more than the map back. I think they want your hide because you broke a code or taboo when buying the map they felt belonged to them. Why the old man chose you to buy the map, I don't know. Probably because a stranger was seen as more gullible than three locals."

"My only thought is to continue on to find the answers at a place marked X, I said with as much conviction I could muster this morning."

In a very short while we had made breakfast and packed up our gear and once more found ourselves on the trail that led us towards our goal. The morning began cool with a persistent wind coming from a far off place. Ever so slowly, the terrain was changing. The thick vegetation was giving was to a more arid setting. We came to a place that springs gushed up and bled down to a plain of sand and mire. This area appeared to be the last place where heavy vegetation grew in the watered way. Since this could be a final place for water Luther and I went forth to fill our water jugs. Feeling the cool sand beneath our feet was pleasant to our senses. Shortly the ooze and water invaded our ankles and calves. Before we knew it, we were caught in the clutches of a place of forbidding quicksand.

Calling out to Sprig and Monty we directed them to not come any closer and to throw us a rope because we were in quicksand. The rope we carried was not long enough to reach us. We were sinking slowly as we both had ceased to struggle and made for a prostrate position by flopping on our bellies. After an indeterminate time that seemed like hours, our favorite young man showed up with a length of vine braided so that it reached us. Monty, throwing the vine rope was just able to reach Luther's fingertips. Luther was first to attempt to reach solid ground. His weight and fastness caused the vines to partially separate several times but held together long enough so that Lunch Box reached a place of safety on terra firma. All the while, I was sinking up to my armpits with the feeling of a giant pulling me down in his tight grasp. Grasping the vine that was cast to me, I used our smaller rope to tie around my chest in case my hands could not hold the vine against the suction of the sand's grip on my body. The advance was slow but sure as inch by inch the sand slowly released its prisoner. When back on solid ground we all lay down exhausted but pleased we had beaten another test of endurance and commitment. What could happen next? We would soon find out.

CHAPTER TWENTY

THE QUICKSAND EVENT left all of us weary and exhausted. We lay on the ground for some period of time before Sprig spoke. "You guys need to get cleaned up and prepare to keep going or we might not get to X this year."

Monty was busy filling our water jugs at a place of solid ground. While Sprig said she would take a short walk away from the springs, Luther and I could fully bathe with complete privacy. The water gushing from the springs was icy cold but was very refreshing; especially knowing our next leg of the journey would take us over desert areas. When all cleaned up the four of us gathered to check the map, consult the compass and Luther used his small sextant to make a sun reading, at noon. All of the readings were in agreement indicating we were on track.

Looking around Luther thought it best to have our noon break here before crossing the terrain ahead. "Not only should our water jugs be full but our stomachs as well," said Luther Lunch Box Locke. We were all in agreement, so that Sprig and Monty moved with economy and haste. All of us enjoyed the hastily prepared repast that would probably have to last us until about sundown if we were to make any good time the rest of this day.

The area did not boast of any visible animals but Monty had said some of these creatures come out at night when it is cooler. Looking ahead it did seem more formidable than any notations on the map. I had lost count of the number of days we traveled thus far. The map indicated a nude land with no trees but not a desert. We traveled all day and the next without any relief from the sun and heat. The region was more desert than I could have imagined. We still had water and food so the going was not so uncomfortable that we wished the trek to end. It was our youth and the hope of finding some kind of treasure at the place marked X that kept us alive and well. Only Monty gave out some disturbing comments from time to time. He was heard to say: "I don't remember this dry place. I thought mountains were close to X." Little remarks like those didn't help the days pass. When asked about those observations he could only answer that he was very young at the time.

Sprig and Luther began to have doubts that spilled over in loud language and heated conversations. I wasn't far behind that position but held my tongue. The excitement was wearing off in this hostile environment. Grumbles began to leak in at every opportunity. Complaining became a fact when marching on new and untraveled terrain. When making camp each night the mood was sullen and somber. We had come to a place of loosing all our manners and enthusiasm. Once or twice, I overheard Luther declaring his desire to, "go back where we belong." I made every effort to sooth the irritations with minimal success. Only Monty kept us all from bickering and pulling out of our goal. (Monty was a mountain of youthful unbridled enthusiasm or naiveté.) He would give hints that we were on the right track and would arrive at our destination in only a few more days. Monty admitted he was not certain if mountains were close to X or if his grandpa circumvented the desert.

"It was a long time ago."

Did Monty change his tune to keep us going? Even with these positive reinforcements, we still stayed in a gloomy mood.

One day it was Sprig with her bright eyes shouted out that some mountains loomed up ahead.

"I see the mountains and know them to be about three days off. Our water is low and out food is near exhausted," said I. Monty piped up and said he could get some food if we would eat snake or lizard. "I catch them if you will eat them."

Our response was unanimous and in unison said: "Go to it, Monty."

That night we dined on desert snake over dried cactus. A banquet back home could not match the delicious offerings that night. We ate to our hearts content. Monty saved the day.

A few days later just as we began to travel into some vegetation an unusual sound came to our ears. It was like a humming but more disturbing in its ominous vibrations. Advancing at a slow and careful pace, again Monty blurted out for us to return to the sands of the fading desert.

"Turn around and leave this place right now, we must go back to sands of desert," he said in a loud and quivering voice. Obeying this command Sprig wanted to know why as well as Luther and I.

"The awful sound you hear is army ants on the move. They eat everything in their path, animal, and plant. Everything! We must get out of here now. They will not march in the sand."

In no time, at all we were racing back to the safety of the sands in the desert. It took about an hour of quick steps to finally avoid the menacing insects and its awful sound. The army ants must send out scouts ahead, because each of us was bitten several times by the hungry critters around the ankles.Looking back to the place we had occupied earlier, we were surprised to see the land completely denuded. We also were startled to see three figures in the distance running out from the forested area at the same time we had left the place. Our only thought was that they were the three amigos still stalking us.

"What on earth are those three trying to do?" Sprig was shaking her finger in that direction as she continued: "They do not seem to be life threatening but annoying as children trying to play a prank on us. The did shoot at Luther with those impotent poisoned arrows."

"They may have been impotent but they still hurt me like the blazes."

"When they ran me into the river they were certainly more than children playing a prank.""Well, I guess what I meant was they seem to act without rhyme or reason. They almost appear to be making it up as they go along."

Monty was looking very knowledgably. "Me thinks they are in the plan to keep you from X. They dress different that other natives in this land. I think they are shaman with much on their minds and are powerful."

"That's all we need are three crazy fanatics with thoughts of magic on their side to continue to harass us."

CHAPTER TWENTY ONE

WITH THE FIRE ants gone and the three stalkers gone we began to slowly advance back into the denuded area to search for jungle vegetation not laid bare by the invading army ants. Hiking first, through the devastated area we made good time. When we finally reached a place where the ants had turned, leaving a large area unscathed we made a midday rest. A few trees were making their stand against the onslaught of natures relentless changes to the land's surface. Under these trees, we found shade and the evidence of water. With these good omens, we enjoyed a happy camp. Monty went on a foray into the unknown and intimidating woods, looking for something better than leftover snake and lizard we had dried earlier. While he was gone, our fire provided us with a pot of steaming hot tea with Sprig's magic touch. The day was warming up but the tea was most welcome. Monty returned with bow and a fat bird that looked a lot like a chicken but with greater plumage and color. Sprig jumped in and had its feathers removed and dressed out so that Luther could skewer it on a spit. While the bird was roasting over the embers of our fire, we began to talk about our situation. Luther was busy with his compass and the map reassuring the group of our success in traveling thus far. "Not too much farther," was his upbeat comment. "Things could be better," was Monty's pronouncement as he finished off the dried snake and lizard of earlier repasts. He also had his portion bird with utterances of satisfaction. A growing boy was our friend and provider.

Looking at the map, I came to the sad conclusion that we were not as close as we had first imagined. Showing the map to Monty, he began to reveal his well-kept secret.

"Grandpa was a real special man. Not like us in the jungle. He once worked at a Coptic Mission. When he was working there, he tried to become a priest. When the brothers confided in him and trusted him, thinking him to be on the way to be a priest, they gave him real religious jobs. When he did this stuff, he found this map and stole it thinking it pointed the way to treasure. He left the priest job and came back home. Later, it was when he took me to the area to find the treasure. When we got to the place, it showed no X at the spot and Grandpa thought the whole thing was just a joke on him to test his trustfulness. Three guards or sentries, like our three boogeymen, were in the area and they sent us back to where we came from with many threats and spooky signs. He made copies for years and sold them to strangers and treasure hunters. The ones he made were false and put the foolish buyers to places far from here. This is the real map because it is the one with the mountains in the background and my fingerprint in the corner that looks like a bush. The other maps did not show the mountains. This place is far from where we lived and where he sold maps. I think we have traveled far and will have to travel some more towards the north."

I was amazed that Monty had that much talk in him as well as his confidence in us to reveal some very pertinent facts we had not known before. I was also pleased with Monty to divulge the truth about his grandpa. Both Sprig and Luther had gravitated to the two of us and heard the bulk of Monty's revelations. Sprig's first impulse was to give Monty a big motherly hug and a kiss on his forehead. Oh to be the recipient of such expressions of love. Would I ever attain that high honor?

Luther winked at me and then said: "We need to pick the young boy's mind to see if any remembrances could give us an advantage on the safety and a way to reduce our destination time." "Let's just take our time to pick his brain. He will tell us when we need to know."

When Sprig had finished her display of affection for our friend she was soon to say. "I think the rest of this tour will be a breeze or at least more fun that the past travels have been."

"Maybe just a breeze but I have a feeling it will be a strong wind if our previous perils are any indication."

"Oh don't be a spoil sport and start to give us the jitters," said Sprig with a gracious smile on her lips and a coyly wink. "We had better move on if we are to ever get to a nice evening camp with good food and a nice rest." Luther was always thinking of food and sleep.

With his advisory, we began our move towards the mountains. The sky was like hammered zinc as we trudged into the thick jungle. The weather was going to change I thought and we had better be prepared. Monty was in the lead, moving with a determined tempo. I hated it to rain on anyone's parade as we were making good time. I will keep an eye on the sky and any unusual breezes before I call a halt to prepare for some possible severe weather. In the jungle, the air became heavy with the smells of rotting vegetation and earthy aromas. Not an unpleasant sensation but it tended to cause one to feel sleepy. The atmosphere became prematurely dark and foreboding with creeping yellow in the clouds. After several hours, it was at this point Monty came back to me and revealed his apprehensions about coming weather. I felt vindicated that my observations were on target with Monty's who had lived in this continent all his life.

"O.K. everybody stop and get ready to hunker down if the coming weather is as severe as Monty and I believe."

"How about food," came the voice of one with a hollow leg?

"We will get fed after we make adequate preparations for the coming storm," I said with thoughts of food on my mind also.

Monty was bending saplings and weaving thatch for a shelter that would be ample for two. Luther and I set up our tent and secured it to some trees close by. When all was secured, Luther broke out some food that was dry and nourishing. Just as all of us had been portioned off with some food, the storm came with an ear splitting crack of thunder and brilliant lightening that seemed to be in our back yard. The entire region quaked at the storm's unleashed fury. "We had made so much progress that the storm is to make us slow down," muttered Sprig as some errant rain ran down her nose. "We certainly are closer to X than we were before the storm," said Luther as he tightened the cover over the food supply. "A couple of days travel should do it if the rain stops so we can move forward without any high water detours."

The storm progressed as though we three did not matter.

CHAPTER TWENTY TWO

THE LIGHTENING GAVE me a sensation of electrifying proportions. The hairs on my arms and head jumped up and tingled. We could all hear a giant tree in the adjacent forest cry out in sickening distress as the lightening bolt split it into two. All around us, the forest shuddered and tried to soak up the torrents of rain on its floor. In a matter of just minutes, the water was starting to try and invade our refuge and the wind was determined to put out our candle. The candle was our only vestige of sanity in this cauldron of nature's retaliation for our invasion into her most sacred wooded sanctuary. We could hear Monty and Sprig's cries of distress and misery as they also fought the invading waters with little success. After a while we called to them to come to our tent for it was holding its own against the mists of heaven. With all four of us in one tent, we had to sit on packs and other supplies. It was close and each calling for the others to not touch the roof or it will start to leak.

"Just move your leg a little, please," was the order of the tent. Monty kept falling off one of the packs to the delight of Sprig who caught him before setting him back on the pack. If it was not howling with torrents of rain outside, we could be said we were having fun.

The storm let up after a few uncomfortable and perspiring hours. It was dark outside so we did not go out and assess any damage to the area. Water was still creeping in the tent via the ground cloth. With wet clothing and disagreeable conditions the best we could do was to doze off for short periods. When morning finally came it was a glorious dawning of sweet proportions of fragrances and cleanliness. We began by placing all of our sodden paraphernalia on bushes to let the rising sun dry them out. Only the great tree off in the forest was showing deadly damage. The stream close by was running bank-to-bank rushing towards the sea to its final destination. We on the other hand still had a destination to reach wet or dry, running or walking. A morning preparation for food was delayed for a while, as each traveler attended to his or her own cleanup and personal belongings modifications. When Luther had made a nice fire with some help from Monty, the camp became brighter to all inhabitants. Dry wood was found in the deadfall of branches in the notches of smaller trees.

"Our food supply has been diminished by the water but we have enough to get us going, with the help of Monty and Dix I would hope for more substantial fare later on," was Sprig's early morning announcement.

She was making coffee that smelled so tantalizing it provided all of us with a renewed hope for better things to come. Moist flour with soda used economically (not to waste rains intrusion) made the flat cakes that stuck to the ribs along with dried fruit that was no loner dry, rounded out our morning sustenance. Honey on the cakes made the packing up a joyous and easy task even with the night's difficulties still on our minds. Luther and I with the help of Monty always at our shoulders gazed at the old map with fresh anticipation.

"My compass reads our goal is almost due north." Luther sounded more positive than in days past. Monty was anxious to get going so we did.

The lad moved ahead with his pack on his back and the machete at the ready as we all melted into the wooded forest. The ground was slushy and muddy in places. Little rivulets still ran in many places trying to rid the forest floor of its excess water. The wetness made the ground springy as we walked over old dead vegetation. The springiness lessened as the morning wore on. Just as we began to approach a slight incline, we heard the voice of Monty giving out a warning. As his cry was fading, I could make his words of warning. "Beware the hole." I didn't see a hole but it was prudent for the rest of us to make a halt at this point and assess what had happened.

"What's going on?" Luther and Sprig said in unison.

"I'm not sure as yet. I heard Monty make a warning about a hole up ahead."

Luther wanted to just move ahead quickly and Sprig wanted us to be quiet in case Monty yelled some more. We became very quiet and cocked our ears towards the front of the trail. We could barely hear Monty giving out a report of warning but we were unable to make out all the words. Sprig was first to break the silence. "I could hear him say he was in hole and for us to be careful when advancing down this incline. Dix, you go first with Luther behind you holding onto your belt and go very slow and careful."

Taking this advice to heart, we advanced slowly until we could hear the young lad's voice more clearly. "At the bottom of the incline there is a hole I fell through. Its dark down here. Please get me out of this hole as I can not climb the walls."

I came to the bottom of this incline and saw no hole unto my foot began to drop into a space that must have swallowed up Monty. Pulling back, we averted any repeat of Monty's predicament. "This is what is called a sink," said Luther with his most authoritative voice. Lunch Box did not squander our time learning together about caving. He went on, "this is what some caves exhibit when the surface sinks into a cave or depression."

"Okay! Cave boy lets get our comrade out of that place as quickly as possible. It can't be any fun in the dark all by ones self." Sprig was already uncoiling the rope to let down into hole.

I advised to make knots in the rope every foot or so because Monty would need them to advance up the rope.

"You people up there be careful not to get too close to the edge because it looks like loose earth. Its very cold down here."

With the knots in place, we lowered the rope to the boy down under. All the while Sprig was giving encouragement and reports on our doings. We felt the rope being tested so Luther and I put the remaining length of rope around our waists for an anchor. At this point, we told Monty to climb out. There was a long pause as we waited for Monty to climb the rope.

"Maybe one of you might want to come down here. It's cold and wet. I think I have found some old objects of peoples long a go as well as a skeleton. This might even be the place marked X.

CHAPTER TWENTY THREE

I T NEVER WAS my intention to go caving on this trip.

"Luther, tie off the extra rope to that small but sturdy tree so I could go down the hole to see what Monty has found."

"Do you think I should go with you?"

"No. Stay up here with Sprig so that she has some protection and company."

"I really don't need a baby sitter for protection but I thank you for thinking of me in that way."

I felt warm all over as Sprig gave me a 'thank you.' Was I silly to try to win over her affections in this dreary setting? When the rope was tied off, I moved to the knotted rope for the climb down. Just as I started to enter the opening, Sprig bent over and kissed my cheek with encouraging words, "be careful, and bring both of you back safely."

This was enough of a surprise so that I replied with the artistry and tact of a great orator. "Yep." It was all I could say.

Hand over hand going down was relative easy using the knots as hand holds. At the bottom was Monty anxiously waiting. He put out his hand to my shoulder and said: "I am happy to see you. Here is the skeleton on the ground."

Looking down with my small flashlight that I had thought to bring with me, I saw a broken and bleached skeleton. The shattered pieces lay in such a way that only the head and hands had any form. Around the neck was a golden chain with a cross of Gothic artistry. On one hand was a wide gold ring. Monty looked at me as if to say: "Are you going to take the cross and ring?" The thought had crossed my mind but in deference to the dead I was all for leaving everything as it was.

Over the sound of the cave's rushing water, I gave out my opinion. "I think we will go up now and leave everything as we found it." Monty seemed relieved as he reached for the rope to make a speedy ascent. Just as I was about to grasp the still dangling rope telling me the boy had reached the top and the arms of one happy Sprig, I swept my flashlight over the wall?An occasional underwater stream that was rushing through this cavern for several millenniums formed this cave. This was a cave entered by an opening somewhere further from this area. The cave was cool in the summer and could be an enticing place for those living in the vicinity, even though in the winter months prolonged dry spells were the norm in this usual arid region. What my flashlight revealed was apparently numerous niches that contained the remains of humans. In the small time period of light, I counted at least eleven recesses. The bones we had discovered had been in an alcove next to the tumbled-in sink that Monty fell through. This was a burial ground for a long period, left undisturbed until the sink gave way after the abnormal heavy rains.

"Hey, Down there! What's taking you so long to climb out? Monty's hoping you leave the ring and cross down there. We don't need that kind of find to take back home." Luther was a good man and a great friend to validate my thoughts exactly.

Sprig was a little more considerate in her comments. "Are you hurt? Can we help in any way? I want to see your face now!"

With these words of motivation, I was up and out of the sink in a matter of seconds. It was in my mind not to divulge anything about the burial ground and its many crypts. I would tell them later when I had sorted out all of my thoughts about this place.

Since the morning was well past high noon, we found a little place off to one side that made a fine to prepare to rest and send Monty out to see if meat could be expected tonight. Sprig and I went in search for berries or fruit that the scrub might offer. Luther remained with the supplies as well as tending to a small fire with water for coffee.

When I was alone with Sprig I began to talk about our futures. "What do you see as your calling in life especially after this escapade?"

"I am not absolutely certain as yet. This trip has been exciting but not as fulfilling as my youth might have longed for. I want something more stable and rewarding to others," said Sprig with as much emphasis as the moment called for.

"I want something more stable too. When we are married we can be very stable together."

"Slow down, Mr. Straight. These things don't happen like they do in romance novels. The process takes time and wisdom."

I know I want all the things you want and I will always be unpredictable but also very stable. Do you want children?"

'Easy Dix. Let's just let the whole idea simmer on a back burner to let the providence of the heavens work out your eager thoughts."

When we found some fruit on a bush we started to pick them for late lunch. I tasted the orbs and found them to be sweet and appealing to the eye. A few berries were added to our outing.

"Don't eat very much of that fruit until we get Monty's O.K. It might not be as good for us as it looks and tastes."Always the wise and careful Sprig. A trait I held in high esteem. On the way back, we tried not to go over any struggling courtship comments or possibilities. Maybe too painful for Sprig?

When we gained the lunch camp, Luther was smiling as he lifted his mug of coffee in our direction. "You two took a long time to gather fruit and berries. I am hungry. Where are the goodies?"

"Has Monty come back as yet? We did get some fruit and berries but we wanted Monty to confine their safety."

"Monty must still be out in the boon docks so have some coffee. I made it fresh and strong."

It was shortly after our coffee clutch that Monty came in with a string of pan—fish.

Luther was first to recognize the importance of this event.

"Get out the frying pan. We are going to eat tonight."

CHAPTER TWENTY FOUR

"I CAUGHT THE FISH in a small lake near-by," said the youthful angler with a casual look of nonchalance, as though it was a daily occurrence and not the act of providing his near starving friends with a banquet. The fire was hot and the fish was prepared for the fry pan. Luther hovered over the feast with the intensity of a fine chef. We used some bacon grease we had saved that was not harmed by the water. The combination of fat and fish set off our salivary glands to high expectations. Sprig gathered what ever was still available in the food department so that when the feast had been devoured we all had our fill.

Afterwards over a second cup of coffee we made plans for the next day's travels. Looking around the dying fire, I noticed Monty also enjoying his coffee as one of us. He had infused himself into our midst as though he was born to be one of us. His expertise in the forest had saved us more than once. I was still in a quandary trying to decide if I should tell the group all that I had found in the bottom of the sink. I noticed Sprig looking at me with that look that women seem to have that says: "Have you told us everything." Maybe she was just staring at me trying to see if I would qualify as good material for marriage. No. She had a sense I had not told all there was to tell about something. I don't know how she did it but her look was enough to turn a lodge initiate into revealing dark secrets. The longer she looked at me I knew I had to tell about the burials in the cave.

"I have to tell you more about what was in the cave back there. The reason I took so long to come up the rope was I saw something. My flashlight on its last sweep of the cave wall revealed a number of niches or recesses in the wall. From what I could see in such a short time were bodies set into each nook, many appearing very ancient. It was surely a Coptic burial vault, since the skeleton on the floor was adorned with a necklace and golden ornate Coptic cross. I knew the area was spooky so I thought it best to wait until we had left that area before revealing this most extraordinary information."

Sprig jumped up and said: "I thought something else was going on down there when you took so long in coming up. What does this mean to us?"

"Don't fret. Cemeteries never caused me to panic or change my ways.

Only Monty," gave no response but his face clouded over with concern.

"What do you think, Monty" was my cautious inquiry. His face deepened with intensity as he began very slowly.

"I think burial grounds very sacred to the peoples of this region. My mind hopes no one in the area is aware of our disturbing of place."

Luther had the answer in mind as he gave his best opinion. "Let's just get as far away from this area as soon as it is convenient so no one can put two and two together."

"The day is far spent but we can still make some headway before dark," said Sprig as she looked like she agreed with Luther.

I had to admit the idea also appealed to me so that in a short time period, after reviewing the map and compass we headed on up the trail towards X. The going was much easier for some reason. I think it is because we were on an established trail, not having to cut our way through any brush or vegetation on the woodsy floor.Just as evening began wash over the sky with clouds of pinks and corals, three antagonists once again assailed us in front of our advancement. The three had on unnerving masks complete with a spear and a branch of pine shaking at us in vigorous threatening gestures. This was the first time the masks were employed and pine branches used as tools to inflict harm. We all stood still and awaited further developments. Only Monty shivered beside me.

The three kept up the threatening for an indefinite time that seemed like hours. They would advance with loud incantations and just as quickly retreat. This went on until they drew up their bows and arrows for even more intense menacing gestures. When this activity had reached a crescendo, Monty put a white cloth on a stick and began to advance towards the three antagonists. This took away the breath of Sprig, who began a pleading for him to return.

"You come back here and wait for us to make a united response to these three native warriors." To Sprig, the three were warriors and yet had never demonstrated to me that they possessed the killing traits of the typical combatant. Watching the young boy moving forward to the wills of the unknown enemy of this escapade made all of us to plead for his immediate return to the safety of our numbers. Try as we might it did not cause the lad the falter in his attempt to negotiate a truce of sorts. The three angry men stopped their machinations to receive the daring boy with the white flag of truce. In no time, the four figures melted into the jungle like cold water running onto hot sand. I had to grab Sprig to keep her from running after the group and its unknown agenda. "I have to go and get Monty and return him to our midst," said Sprig with that feminine determination in her voice that was now quite established in her personality.

"Monty can take care of himself just like he has demonstrated many times on this trip," I responded.

Luther jumped in with his observation: "He must have had something in mind when he offered up the flag of truce. Monty is one young man that does not waste time or effort. I'm sure he will return with more good news than bad."

It was a comfort to hear Luther divulge his inner assessment of the boy's qualities. He had some reservations about the youngster when we first began the adventure. He saw what I saw, a mature man in a boy's body.

"Well you can admire him all you want but he is still a boy. I am going in after him with a gun if he is not returned in exactly one hour. I hope you are with me. Nevertheless, if not I will go alone."

CHAPTER TWENTY FIVE

W E SPENT THE time waiting, looking at our watches, and breaking out any food to nibble on. The day was well spent with evening coming on and its uncompromising darkness. When Sprig noticed this was happening before the hour would be up she looked at Luther and said: "Give me your Gun. I'm going in before the hour is up." Luther looked at me with quizzical eyes that spoke of chivalry and logic. "What do you think Dix?"

"You don't need his permission to give your gun to me. I am going in with or without you, or the gun"

"I think it is a bad idea, but it beats sitting around here waiting for something to happen. We all should go.'

"Well let's get started."

"We should pack up our gear to protect it from anyone or thing while we are gone. It will only take a minute."

"You pack up then while Luther and I get on the trial of those three plus see what has happened to Monty."

"OK but be very careful. I think those three are up to no good. They seem to represent villainous and odious behavior."

The words were barely out of my mouth when Luther and Sprig disappeared into the jungle at the same place Monty went in with three pathetic losers. This left me with the chore of packing up the gear all but the paraphernalia that we would need for an overnight.

I began to think of the danger the boy and Sprig had taken by going into that jungle with only Luther as the safety officer. My eyes and gun would have doubled their ability for protection in that unknown environment. Sprig had certainly attached herself emotionally to Monty. Maybe it was a strong mother instinct. That would be good for us later. That thought brought up the question about her attraction to me. Was I missing any subliminal signals about her feelings towards me? Maybe I should not be so forward in my assumptions about her marrying me, vocally. My mouth had always been the telegraph of my feelings. Maybe this was not the time to express myself so ardently to her tender ears and personality. I suppose my comments should be just natural and let things take their normal course and not force anything. This would be my most intelligent conviction at this time.To my surprise, after these deep thoughts that distracted me from my surroundings the time had moved on at rapid pace. I was roused from my deep thoughts as the group of six came out from the forest. The three scoundrels leading the way with the up-raised white cloth of peace and safety. I thought the time had been brief but when I looked at my watch and saw the moon rising in a darkened sky, I became aware that some extensive time had elapsed, since their departure. Monty and Luther brought up the rear with Sprig still holding the gun on the advance of the three. I guess a parley was in order now. Sprig was the first to speak.

"We all have had a nice informative meeting in the deep forest that clears up a lot of things. Monty was able to converse with the three and then translated to me in his best English. Get a fire up and blazing for some food for all of us and maybe break out some tea. When we have eaten and are refreshed, I will try to explain all to you. Our three friends, I believe no longer require felonious scrutiny for their explanations vindicate their actions."

Luther also was excited and wanted to reveal some things but Sprig gave him 'the Look.' Luther could only say: "Dix, you will be surprised and amazed at the unfolding of this revelation about our three friends." Sprig added quickly, "we had best get some food and rest our bodies for a time of revealing and counseling."

The water for tea was ready and we finished up some fish and Johnnycakes to everyone's delight. The three young men ate with a relish that surprised me. They must not have eaten for quite spell. When all the food was consumed, Sprig stood up and began to disclose all she had learned from the questionable three. Monty beamed as Sprig spoke. "We found out what and who these gentlemen are. They belong to a group or family that had been assigned the task of repelling all people or strangers from this particular area. Dix, you were singled out originally because you had purchased the real map from Monty's grandpa. That map had been in the possession of the Coptic's for centuries and kept in a place where no one could get to it. Monty's kin stole the map by hook or crook after being rejected as a future Coptic priest in that place marked X. When the map was out of the control and jurisdiction of the family that guarded the secret place they were tasked to find it and return it at all costs. This actually was years ago that the family was told to get the map back. These three had not been born yet. The duty of guarding this location had been handed down from generation to generation for about two thousand years. Their family or group had been delegated to guard this place on the map with all due diligence and tenacity, this included hurt and harm if need be. When we became a threat to the region, they changed their tactics somewhat. Threatening to get us to leave the area and give up the search was what they wanted us to do. In desperation, they sneaked up to one of our camps at night and tried to listen to our conversations. They heard us call out my name and knew that it was one of the signs they were looking for. They had been told to be on the lookout for a young boy and a maiden, to permit them access to the X sight. They had been told to use Noah's actions as their guide. One coming out of the wilderness. The family had been told centuries before to be on the lookout for two signs before they could give up guarding the X sight. The clincher was when Monty revealed his real name. A biblical name. They became excited and wanted to lead us to the sight right away. The signs came from the bible. When we examine the sight the three will tell us what to do next. So let's get a good night's sleep and start out early in the morning."

Looking up and scanning the campsite, we were all perplexed to find the three native young men had quickly excited the camp. With some sputtering from Luther who tried to prolong the revelations, we exited to our respective sleep quarters.

We had given Sprig our ground cloth for a makeshift tent and Monty preferred to sleep out side. An excited camp tried to find sleep as the night's sounds surrounded us with only a benign din.

CHAPTER TWENTY SIX

SINCE WE COULD do nothing about the absence of the three, we prepared to get some sleep with faint knowledge that the three natives in the jungle forest would not attack us. The night passed quickly with only a few questions bandied about my head before the sandman came to bring rest and sleep.

In the morning we had nothing to eat, so we made a strong brew of tea to see us through the rigors of starting out on our final trek. We had more to travel than we first thought because the map was not drawn to scale. The three said that we should continue to follow the map because we will need the confidence to continue the search. What ever that meant. Sipping the hot tea, Sprig was soothed into more explanations about the real name of Monty and the significance of her name, Sprig.

"Well, it is most the unique explanation about the names and the action of Noah that these three had been indoctrinated. The keepers of the Coptic sight, which X indicates, had the signs about whom they should let into the ruins of the old Coptic ruin. 'Look for the action o Noah, had been their validation of who to permit access to the ruin. Monty's real name is Joseph Angel Dove and mine is Sprig. That was what Noah evidenced when he sent out the Dove to determine if the land was safe to occupy. When the dove brought back a sprig of the olive tree Noah was sure that it was safe to exit the ark and venture forth. These two names are a fulfillment of their centuries old assignment to protect the Coptic Church from unauthorized occupation. Therefore we can go forward looking for a church ruin without the threat of three defenders of the sight."

That is a long explanation and most unique. With all this clarification of events, what do you think the old Church sight has to offer us?" Luther had been hoping for riches that usually are not found in Coptic churches, whether old or new.

"It now appears we have a long way to go yet so lets get going while Monty searches for some food along the way." The Lunch Box was on empty so food was still on his mind.I could only add: "We are still headed for the distant mountains that could be ten miles or one hundred miles ahead. We will traverse some foothills before we ever get to the mountains." Sprig jumped in with her upbeat and positive remark. "If we don't complain about the circumstances we will find the going more enjoyable and the time yielding almost effortlessly."

Packing up and heading out was robot-like, as we had gone through the motions time and time again until we had perfected the procedure.

Monty or Joseph Angel Dove was in the lead as usual but now a very happy boy that found himself in the center of a very special event. Angel Dove went off in the brush after a while only to return in a short interval with a chicken-like bird that we soon dressed it and cooked it over a small fire. The bird was delicious. He had also found some berries that we used for more tea. Since we were refreshed, we decide to skip a noonday halt and just keep going at a breakneck speed. How were we to know we had come close to the X? Sprig had informed us earlier that we would know by some geographical feature that would stand out and disclose our objective. With this in mind, we covered a lot of ground before the evening sky began its westward sinking. We setup camp before the night fell on us. Angel Dove had gone off again on his foray into the brush all about us. The land about us was beginning to thin out. When he returned his catch was a half dozen of the largest frogs, I had ever seen.

"A small pond is just over that small hill were many tasty frogs live."

I was certain that Monty knew the difference between good frog and poison frogs. Luther pounced on the amphibians with a zeal that would embarrass a lightening strike. A fire was ready when the frog legs were available. We had only a small amount of oil to fry them in but the result was pure ambrosia. This along with more tea made from this morning's berry supply, once again gave us the sustenance we needed. It reminded me of the manna in the wilderness. We had just enough for today and tomorrow will bring us just enough to keep us going to the promised sight.

We spent the rest of the evening going over all the things the three had told Angel Dove to make sure we had not jumped to any conclusion not backed by logic or faith. Sprig sat close to me as we went over every detail concerning the adventure. I made some comments that I hope would further my standing in the eyes of an olive branch.

"I think this whole affair is about some biblical phenomena that have some importance that we are unaware of at this time. The thing about Noah is very unusual to be used in this modern age. We now have radios, airplanes, and other modern things to relate everything biblical to the whole world. What could be so special that a family has guarded a site for so many generations? No one has stumbled onto this site is very unusual. Now a today's people are everywhere doing every thing. Nothing seems to be hidden anymore. Even King Tut's tomb has been found. The fact that a dove and a sprig together on a search like this must be an astronomical coincidence."

"I don't know how many days we have traveled but I sense we are getting closer to our goal." Sprig's positive comment was a good one to end the night's discussion.

Luther was ready for sleep as he bubbled out about the next day. "We can try and found some more grub to keep body and soul together. I will try my luck along with Monty so we can at least arrive on a full stomach. These rations do leave one to dream about sumptuous banquets." With these visions dancing in our heads, we all adjourned to our sleep quarters.

CHAPTER TWENTY SEVEN

THE NIGHT CONCLUDED without any adverse incidents. We all slept this night without posting any guards. I slept fitfully because of my thoughts of danger in the night with or without the three former antagonists assuring us that, they would keep a cautious eye on our whereabouts. The morning came with clever little clouds escorting a vivid blue sky for those of us up at this early hour. My job was to wake the sleepy heads and get the camp up and running. I took a certain amount of pleasure in this task. "O.K. Lunch Box you can't eat your breakfast while still in the sack." Even though I knew, our breakfast would again be sparse. Frog legs and chicken wings left over from Monty's marvelous abilities to get food when we needed it. "Luther will you go out and see if you can get some fish or frogs to assuage our hunger?" I was vaguely aware that Angel Dove or Monty as he preferred to be called by us, was not in his blankets. The lad was always up first in our group so I thought little of it. When he returned this time, it was with a string of Fish. Tiger fish he called them. With Sprig and Luther up and in active mode it was only a short time before a fire was burning nicely. Monty supplied some green sticks to impale the fat little fish for roasting over the fire. Enough berries from yesterday gave the coffee pot its honor to supply us with hot water for some delicious tea. When the breakfast club had finished and all supplies once more packed up we left this little oasis in the sparsely forested area.As we traveled north, it became apparent to all of us that the foliage became meager to the dismay of us all. Little shade from the ever-present blazing sun. Trees gave way to shrubs that we noted to be full of hostile needle-like thorns. The earth beneath our shoes became more and more sandy. That made our advance more difficult. We noticed at once that the river that we had encountered days ago now presented its self in the distance as a wide and muddy channel racing towards its final destination. The river was far away and looked like a brown ribbon trying to escape to its end, the sea. Squinting through the sun's persistent out pouring of heat and light we became chagrined when we noticed the slavers boat on the river, going down stream towards the sea.

"There is the bunch that captured us trying to make us expensive fodder for their slave business. I was hoping we had put them out of business but from here, it looks like they have captured a few unfortunate beings. We had better be sure and shy a way from those brigands.""Now Dix.You mean we cannot try and free those people before we continue on?" It appeared that Sprig was set on being the catalyst for freeing those people down below. The unscrupulous slavers had caught those folks and put them at a great disadvantage because of their fear and bonds. I knew we could not talk her out of her wish to be a savior to those less fortunate than ourselves and I found myself readily concurring.

"Luther, do you have a plan?"

"The best plans I know of is to ask Monty if we can count on the three amigos and does he have any suggestions?"

These circumstances require someone more familiar with this situation than we three outsiders."

All this time Monty was listening with youthful enthusiasm and regard. "We can overtake them and free my people with little trouble. I see only four villains guarding the captured tribal peoples like myself. The slavers must have taken the people by deception and practiced stealth. I am positive that the three amigos, as you like to call them, are fully aware of our situation and would be more than capable to help us if and when they are needed."

"Well I can feel that you are right but do we have an actual plan to overtake the slavers and free those people? My concern is that we only have one gun left over from our previous troubles. Making us vulnerable to any weapons they four slavers might have," I commented with a degree of hesitancy in my voice. Luther came to my rescue. "I think what Dix is trying to say is we have to be very careful and positive in our plans before we put into action what we envision in our minds."

"Thanks Luther. What are your thoughts about a rescue Miss Sprig?

"Well, for one thing we should not put Monty in danger in any way shape or form. I can hold up any part of any plan you devise regardless of danger or risk." What a woman I thought, as we began to formulate the action needed to overtake the slavers and free the captured peoples.

Monty in his high-pitched youthful voice began to outline his thinking on this venture.

"We need to have a happening that would take the guards attention away from their captives. I can do that if we get close enough without discovery. I will make loud and fierce noises of beasties that are known to attack people.

When they are looking my way you will either free the people or make the slavers useless blobs of flesh."

"Sounds like a plan to me," said Luther with his usual casual comments in the face of danger.

"I will find some clubs if I can in this desolated place so we can clobber the villains," said Sprig with some doubt as to where she could find clubs in a short time we need to affect the plan. Monty was looking at us and had a quizzical expression on his face. "I don't have hose on my feet but all of you have foot hose. If you take them off and fill them with sand we could us them to wield as fine knocker weapons. They can put one to sleep with one sock, without making a sound."

Sprig was first to recognize this suggestion as the best contribution thus far towards the plan to free the enslaved, especially since no clubs were forthcoming in this desert-like area. "Bravo, young lad. We find that your contributions to our causes have become constant and brilliant. We love you for who you are and for also what you have done." The boy-man face beamed like the sun as he slowly took in the compliment coming from one that he loved too.

Where was I during this time of compliments and visions of love from both of my close friends? I stood back and just enjoyed the camaraderie of two of the best friends Luther and I could ever ask for.

Luther was champing at the bit. "Lets mosey on down the sand dune to intersect this little group and let Monty make with the noises so we can discombobulate the slavers."

Without another word, we had removed our socks and filled them with sand. With our shoes back on we carefully edged our way down the sand dune towards our unwary Prey.

CHAPTER TWENTY EIGHT

Traveling on the sandy terrain was difficult and tiresome. We didn't want our quarry to see us so we had hunch down as well as fight the unstable sand. The stream did have some thick foliage to help to cover our approach. The distance did eventually became close enough that Monty signaled us to move to one side and a little closer before he began his attempt to roar like a lion or was it to yap like wild dogs. We would just have to wait and marvel as his ingenuity and divers talents.

With no warning, our little friend began his animalistic sounds of roaring and barking all at once. This caused the slavers to stop and look in that direction. The slaves were not frightened knowing the sounds came from one of their own. When the slavers all turned to investigate the sound, the three of us were capable of boarding and swinging our sand-socks to render the four villains unconscious. The slaves began to chant a song of redemption as Monty on board to help in the untying of the little group of captives. Monty was able to explain about their situation and that they were free to return home. The area was soon void of all the recent past of captivity and despair. The boat was made fast to prevent its departure. The slaves wanted to take the slavers on a one-way trek but after awhile Monty was able to discourage that eventuality. They let us have them.

Caring the unconscious villains back to the moored boat was not an easy task. Luther was able to carry one on each shoulder so I tried to duplicate the task. My body was wearing out as we traveled over the sand to the boat. Sprig and Monty were in unison pulling the last slaver down to the river with about as much difficulty as I was having. When all the evil flesh was aboard, luckily, it still floated; we set the craft adrift toward the sea.

We assembled ourselves to continue our excursion to a place in the desert foothills where X must be. It was mostly uphill and very arduous. The mountains in the distance caused the moisture-laden clouds to rise so they could pass over the mountains. In doing so they expended all the rain on the far side leaving this side nearly desolate of moisture. This caused this small region to be a desert on the edge of the previous jungle. The clouds gathered moisture from the sea close by and went on by the winds to rain on the forest we had just departed.

Looking at the map and compass, we all surmised that X was close by. Luther began to climb up a sand dune and at the top; he was surprised to find a ruin of some ample proportions.

"This has got to be it," shouted one excited Luther Locke. The structure was filled in with sand, but one could still ascertain it had been a church by the Coptic crosses in the walls. One large cross was still visible where the altar must have been. A remnant of a lectern was also at that end on the structure.

"Where do we begin," ejaculated Sprig in a high state of anticipation.

"We begin at the beginning," said I with certain flair of the obvious. "Does the map show any structure and a special place of X?"

I had looked at the map many times but never really scrutinized the place marked with the X. The X marks the spot was all I had seen.

"Yes," said Luther holding the map at arms length. "The X is contained in a small rectangle at the far end of the small diagram that would correspond to the place under the wall with the Coptic Cross."

We all gathered at that spot to see if any telltale signs were to be found. As we were looking, down at the rubble around the corner came three young geezers that had recently been our antagonists. With smiles and gestures of greetings, they all pointed down at the rubble and made motions of digging. Kneeling down we began to remove debris and rubble. When we took a minute to rest, it was noticed by all of us that the three amigos had once more vanished. Only Monty didn't seem surprised. "They will return once we have found the thing that has been protected by their family for centuries. We are now under their protection and instructions. With assurance from someone that should know, we continued to clear away the remnants of the wall and other parts of the structure. This place had to be a thousand years or older I thought, according to what the three had said about how many generations their family had been commissioned to guard and protect this small real estate.

A sudden squeal of discovery came from Sprig as a trap door appeared beneath the place they had excavated. "Look! This must be where the object of our search rests just under this portal. We need a tool to pry open this last obstacle."

Monty was on the ball as he found the shovel the three had left behind for us to use as we saw fit. With Luther doing the honors, he pried open the door. The void revealed was complete with steps going down. At the bottom was a pile of desiccated animal skins of various origins. Badger skins and lamb's skins were all wrapped around an object. Luther descended and handed me a bundle. I pulled the bundle of fragile and delicate wrappings out of its resting place and moved up and to a more conducive place for examination on the surface. On one of the remaining half-standing walls, we placed the bundle and began the laborious exercise of unwrapping the object. The skins fell away as dust and revealed a ceramic-like container of no real value. I held it up so all could see and try and to figure out its importance. One family had for two thousand years protected this area so no one could desecrate it or unearth this object before us. "What are we to do now," said Sprig with sort of sadness in here voice since we had searched and found X without the normal jubilation of finder's keeper's. She looked like she wanted to return the bowl or basin back in its resting place and just find a way back to her Father's mission. Luther had noticed some figures on the object and was trying to figure out the meaning. "These are not figures but are ancient letters. It is most probably Greek. We may have found a relic that has more value then we can imagine. If only I had studied my ancient languages more diligently I might decipher the meanings of this artifact."

The round artifact was made of hand carved stone or ceramic with some silver on its upper edge that appeared very black. This had been in the house of some well—to-do family or person long ago. I tried to read the inscription with no more success than Luther. We would have to gingerly clean the basin to bring out the script more clearly. Apparently, we had the time and the protection to be at ease in this our final search to translate the inscription. Would it lead us further or would it be a dead end without resolution or conclusion?

CHAPTER TWENTY NINE

A FTER SO MUCH excitement, we opted for making a camp nearby and getting some food and rest before continuing in our revelation pursuit. Off to one side was a small depression that afforded us some protection and coolness with its marvelous grassy blanket. Here too we found a seep of water that afforded us some respite from the relentless sun and constant desert wind.Sticks were in small supply, so Monty went on a tour of the entire surrounding area looking for some fuel for our wee fire. Just when I thought I would go and look for our young partner he came up the dune with an armful of twigs and sticks, enough for a fire that would cook our meal and heat our water. Looking past Monty I saw the three Amigos coming up the dune with some more firewood in hand. When they all reached the camp, we were surprised to see that the Three offered us three birds looking like regular chickens for cooking. After dressing the birds, we dipped them in some boiling hot water in a half jug we dressed the birds to remove the innards and feathers, then the birds were ready for roasting over our ember-laden fire. The hot coals singed the last of the hairy feathers on the birds and began the roasting with pleasant aromas only roasted meat could emit. The three Amigos had gathered some roots that were edible so we proceeded to boil them in more hot water until tender. When this repast was ready, we all sat down in a circle and ate our fill with little talking. Afterwards the circle turned into a round discussion group. The comments turned to the item found in the old Coptic ruin. Sprig had taken the bowl and with water from the seep, had cleaned up the relic so that we could examine it more closely. The inscription was in Greek so that Luther and I could make some sense of it.

"Basically it names the probable owner of the bowl. It looks like Joseph of Jerusalem and was given to the Coptics here by Apostle John Mark. In small letters scratched in, which were more or less added later, is the name of Yeshua of Nazareth. From my Bible days, it might appear we have the basin Jesus used to wash the apostles feet before the last supper. This gift to the Coptics was by way of John Mark the Apostle and evangelist when he established the Orthodox Coptic Church in this part of the world. The Coptics must have hidden the relic so that the influx of opposing religions would not destroy it. You can see the damage done to this church millenniums ago probably by angry new converts to other religions. With this in mind it will be our duty to be very diligent when we again begin to travel out of here "

"Now that we have found it what are we going to do with it?" Sprig was thinking ahead to the next part of our expedition.

Just then, Monty piped up and said: "The three guards want to tell you something. The best I can translate is that you must now take the bowl to Jerusalem and wait by a place called the Damascus gate and await for further instructions."The three Young Geezers tried to tell Monty more but had a hard time making Monty understand. "They say you must wait by this gate until two young men approach you and ask if you need water for your bowl, even though you will have it concealed. At that point, you must give the two young men the bowl and then leave the area."

"Well that sounds interesting and how are we going to get to Jerusalem? I am tired and clothes hungry and wanting a more substantial food menu," blurted Luther of Lunch Box fame.

Luther was always thinking of culinary delights. Sprig was on her feet with the answer to our problems. "If we can get to the coast and find a town with a radio I can radio Dad for money and clothes so we can continue our adventure to the conclusion. Randall could fly up in the mission's plane and land in any small space. I know that going up to Jerusalem is very important to us and maybe the world."

Sprig was always positive and primed for more exciting exploits. She stood straight and firm in her conviction that we could do this and be happy doing it. I will marry this girl, and spend my life with her if only she would recognize me as a viable suitor.

It wasn't long before we formulated a plan of action that included Monty if he wanted to go with us. Our discussion went on for a long time and while we were intent on the particulars, the Three Amigos stealthily melted from our midst without any noise or good byes. I suppose its better this way.Our plan consisted of wrapping the bowl and placing it in Luther's backpack. We then cleaned up the campsite and prepared to sleep. The night was warm and balmy so that we did not set up any enclosures but just slept on the grassy ground. Wrapped in our blankets for extra comfort and a feeling of safety, we became drowsy as the embers of our dying fire flickered and fluttered into oblivion.I could think of a thousand reasons to end the search now and return the bowl to some museum and go on to live normal lives. With Luther snoring, I hazarded a chance to whisper to Sprig some of my thoughts.

"Sprig, do you still want to get married to me when this search is over?" The night enclosed itself around my words so that I thought she had not heard. After a period of time I strained to listen for any sounds, I was surprised to hear Sprig's small feminine voice penetrate the night's gloom.

"You don't know what you would be getting into my friend. My whole family is a little weird. I want to get married sometime and will know when that sometime has arrived. Just be patient, my friend, for now. Our time will come later. I feel a great tugging now of going to Jerusalem even if the area is in turmoil.

My heart pounded at the words of possibilities smothered me in a warm and fuzzy nostrum. Sleep came quickly as the visions poured over my brain. The morning came brightly with blue skies and birds singing somewhere off in the distance.

CHAPTER THIRTY

IN THE MORNING, we were not surprised to notice that the three guards had left the area for parts unknown and had not made contact with any of us. We fixed some breakfast in an almost mechanical manner since we had completed this exercise many times before. Each one fell to their appointed chores so that all was prepared in a short time.

Moving out with the ancient basin securely wrapped with some of Luther's clothing we set out to the east to meet the coast and find some small fishing village so Sprig could radio her Dad. If Dad and Randall could carry out what Sprig had in mind, our search would take on a new meaning and direction. We had left our passports at the mission and would ask Dad to send them along. Only Monty would not have any passport so we would have to cross the border in a clandestine manner or be imprisoned.

When reaching the coast we did not see any villages at this point. It seemed prudent to travel towards the place we imagined the little river we had seen a few days ago would empty in the larger body of water, probably the Red Sea. This logic was rewarded soon after we began our coastal trek. A small fishing village appeared ahead with only a few shacks and buildings to give us hope for a radio and a small airfield. Approaching the village with caution, we had split up into two groups of two each. Sprig and I came across a small but sturdy building at the edge of the fishing village that appeared to be some sort of official structure. True to our desires, it was also at a point on a small airfield. What luck we had still held. Monty and Luther came upon the scene just as we knocked on the door of the little building. Monty and Luther stayed back from the door around a corner to render assistance if any were needed.

A sleepy looking local with a sort of uniform came to the door and as he opened it, he demanded what we wanted during his siesta time. When he finally focused on us, he became more alert as he said: "What are two gringos doing in this part of the world?" Calling out to his comrade, he opened the door wider to permit us to enter. "Hey, Pablo, look what we have here at our humble abode." With this, Pablo came forward sleepy-eyed but carrying a rifle for effect. "What do you want, here?"

Sprig tried telling of our misadventures and a need to contact her father to bring aid to our little party. "Do you have a radio here that I could use to contact my father at the Gardener Mission in the south?"

"Is your father the missionary there that treats the natives and helps the miners down there?""Yes. He is Herb Gardener of the Mission of Good Deeds that is a medical outpost."

"In that case you can use our radio to contact him. We have heard of his good works up here ever since he came to this region."

"Is this out post having a serviceable airstrip for our people to land a small plane when bringing us supplies?"The first man answered with a wave of his hand. "You can see it behind us but we can't guarantee its worthiness. It might need a few repairs before we could call it safe."

"What kind of repairs does the strip need?" Sprig asked as she held out her arms and hunched her shoulders in very typical gesture she used to get more information from her listeners. This startled the two men, that we supposed were in the governments employ, to list a number of airstrip hazards that needed to be set right before a plane could land safely.

"There are holes and stubby brush and some limbs as well as old muddy places that need to fixed. Maybe you can hire some local men to assist you in repairing the strip. Pablo and I must stay on alert to observe any slavers or brigands in the area. So your time on the radio must be very short in case we need to report these events to our central government."

I knew we must also find a boat or ship going north that would take us on up the canal and ultimately to Palestine.

"Do ships come by here often that we could board for a journey north?"

My question surprised the two men.

"Why would you want to go north and into dangerous areas?"

Sprig was smart enough to interrupt and ask permission to see the radio and try to raise her father.

I left the building and joined Luther and Monty telling them of the events and that we need to seek out some local men to help with the airstrip repair. Monty reminded us of the siesta time and no one would venture out at this time of the day. Therefore, we agreed to wait for Sprig's radio call for help from her father. In the meantime, we found some shade under a tree, waited, and rested in the little village that was also inactive and resting. Only Luther seemed to feel uneasy in our present situation and he said so.

"This village and the two men inside give me the creeps."

"What exactly gives you the creeps?"

'This village is too quiet and the two men are too eager to get us to enlist some locals to refurbish their airstrip. Why haven't the two kept up the landing strip themselves?"

Monty was throwing stones at some imaginary target as he stood up to look down the main street for any life or movement. "Most times one could see a dog or even an old man in a chair resting on the front veranda where it would be cooler than inside the house."

I think the people have been sent away or this town has been ravaged by the slavers with the consent of the two officials in the air strip tower."

'That's a harsh assessment, Monty," said Luther with an additional scan of the village to justify Monty's suspicions. 'You have to admit, Dix, Monty's observation is probably on target once again. I see no movement or hear a sound of any kind that would reveal a vibrant village, not even smoke from the chimneys. We will have to be very careful as we spend time in this area. I am going back to check up on Sprig and her attempt to contact her dad at the mission."

Good idea, Luther. While you are gone, Monty and I shall amble around the residences and see we find ant signs of life. Let's meet back here in 30 minutes for a conference on how to go forward from these circumstances."

Luther moved towards the brick building that housed the two officials while Monty and I started down the street actually hugging the verandas on one side for a better inspection of both sides of the avenue. No dogs and no old men in chairs tilted back on the verandas snoozing away the siesta. Looking into doors and windows no one was observed. This village was deserted and bare as the tomb.

CHAPTER THIRTY ONE

ETURNING TO THE government building, Monty and I met Sprig and Luther coming out of the place. They both appeared to be full of information and I was eager to tell them about the vacant village.

"I got through to dad and he is going have Randall fly up here with clothes and passports and money for our next leg of our search. He was very chagrined that we were not coming home. I didn't tell him out final destination or our find because he would have left our passports at home."The two government men told us all about the slavers coming through town causing the villagers to flee into the bush. The people should return shortly, according to the two G men. The villagers will be very willing to help in the reconditioning of the airstrip because they love to see airplanes, according to our two G men. Tools are to be found in the little shed out in the back. Shovels, picks scythes etc. will be needed to fix up the landing strip."

"Monty and I went into the village and can verify no one is at home. What we need now is some food and water to sustain us in this task. Maybe when the people return we can entreat them for a few vittles to keep us fit for the job ahead."

"Sounds like a plan," said Luther as he rubbed his tummy as it made gastric grumbling sounds.

Reaching the little shed we pulled out the necessary tools for the job ahead. Most of the implements looked like they hadn't been used in years. Luther and I began to oil and sharpen them with a file and sand block. When we had finished the voice of Monty was first to announce the return of local villagers. With the thought of food on our minds, Luther said he would go and try to reason with some of the people to share a morsel or two with us before we reconditioned the airstrip. He was gone in a flash with Monty on his heels. I thought they must be hungrier than they had indicated earlier in the day. Sprig and I brought up the rear with smiles on our faces reflecting our common assessment of Luther and Monty as childlike but very open in their contact with life.

"Come on in!" Luther was standing on the first large porch he had come to and waved his arms in a most excited manner. "They have some food they want to share with us and to help in the maintenance or the landing field."Luther with his flashing smile and silver tongue had no trouble with these folks to share with us and to be happy doing it. His Spanish was more than passable. He was sitting on a bench next to the table with Monty, raising his hand with what looked like a giant tortilla with meat running out the sides. Monty sat close to Luther and held a smaller version.

The lady of the house was most emphatic as she waved us to sit down and begin eating her offerings. "Sit. Sit." Her English was very good. "We have plenty of food here since living in the bush for several days. I wanted to heat up the food but your friends were so hungry they just started eating. We think it was you that sent the slavers out to sea and away from here. Because of that we want to be of service to the four of you."

Sprig and I allowed the good lady to heat up our food on a small charcoal brazier. We waited some time before our food was heated to her satisfaction. Monty and Luther said they would go up and begin the chore of repairing the airstrip. The man of the house went with them after rounding up about five six other villagers to help. The lady of the house opened up with all the news about her village and the two G men. "Those two government men are lazy and probably encouraged the slavers to come into the village. Thanks be to God none from here was taken and sold into slavery."

"Can you tell us anything else about the town and the local sea port as well as the airport?"

"Not much to tell. The seaport has about three ships a month coming in to offload supplies and take away cotton that we raise. We also have grapes and pomegranates to ship out as well as wheat. We are blessed with at least two growing seasons in this climate. The ships take lumber up the coast and return to take our goods up the coast the coast. "The airstrip is rarely used because of the poverty of the country and our people. Maybe if we repair the landing strip the two men in charge will request more planes to come in with tourists or urgent supplies instead of waiting weeks for special merchandise."

"Well we hope to have a plane come in tomorrow with more clothes and food for the four of us," said Sprig as she demonstrated her tattered and torn clothes to the lady with the good English and food. Magda was the name of the lady of the house and she was trying to convince Sprig to take some clothes from her.

'I have some clothes that will fit you if we can reduce the size by sewing and stitching."

"I thank you for the offer but we all shall have our own clothes when my father sends the airplane here with supplies and clothes. I think we must go and help in the repairing of the strip. It was very good of you to feed us with your good food and hospitality. We are very grateful."

Sprig and I left the home of Magda with the lady smiling and waving as we made our way up the road to the airstrip. The day was hot and dusty with little dirt devils popping up on the bare parts of the airfield. The group that was working had made a lot of progress towards making the field serviceable. Sprig and I each grabbed a tool and begin the task of filling in the depressed pockets

"I sure hope this field will be good enough for Randall to land without any mishaps," said Sprig as she wielded the shovel with a practiced hand that was a wonderful addendum to her talents.

My hope was that Randall was not anything to Sprig but her father's helper. I'll find out when he comes in from the mission as the savior of our little group. From the village came the call to come in out of the hot sun and rest by partaking of cool beverages. Magna had a voice that could be utilized as a tornado warning horn.

"Everyone come down and rest. You have been out in the sun long enough. I have cool beverages for all."

We all came without the need of a second call. Monty led the way with Luther on his heels.

CHAPTER THIRTY TWO

SITTING IN THE shade and talking to the local folks, and sipping cool beverages I could almost forget the difficult situation we were in. We were in a strange land with a historic relic that these people no doubt cherished. We were broke and untidy. With little protection, we were at the mercy of all the peoples around us. If the slavers reinforced themselves and returned to this village, we would have a tough time of it. All of our hopes were riding on Randall and his arrival with supplies, clothes, passports, and funds.

Luther was in a lively conversation with one of the locals. The subject was about the airstrip. Luther wanted to continue working on it in the cool of the evening but the local thought the strip was good enough to land an airplane. Eventually, Luther came to me and said," we had better get up to the strip and finish our work. We don't want Randall to crack up on landing." I had to agree.

"Get Monty and Sprig's attention and let's continue to work on the field."

As we got up and headed back to the field most of the others followed us with their tools without complaining.

The only one left behind was Luther's earlier contentious conversationalist. He made a beeline for the coast and the ships' docks.

Our little group was met by one of the officials who gave us the news that Randal had left the mission and would arrive early in the morning. They also told us that they had heard from their superiors who ordered them to detain us until our passports arrived and to notify the Capital of any irregularities. At this news, the four of us were ushered into the brick building and placed in a holding room. The locals that had accompanied us thus far indicted they would continue to work on the field until they were satisfied that it was good enough to land an airplane.

The room was small and barren with only a small window that looked out on the airstrip. Instead of chairs, we had to sit on some quaint, hard wood benches next to a simple table. When we were seated, Luther looked out the window to find the locals continuing the work on the airfield; afterwards we had a council of war. The relic was safe so far and the two G men had not been cruel or belligerent. Something we were all thankful for. Luther had kept his pack close to him for security and protection. No one seemed to be very inquisitive about Luther's pack and his seemingly over protective stance concerning his backpack. His protective demeanor concerning the pack was only apparent to us, I guess. The rest of us had left our backpacks here in the brick building.

"We certainly need to have some backup plans about getting out of here and going on to Jerusalem," I said.

"This confinement complicates our entire momentum to finish this search," Sprig said with a slight weariness in her voice. Her eyes also looked tired but beautiful. We were all tired but found it impossible to find a comfortable spot to nap or sleep. Luther kept us informed as to the events out side the little window. "The men are still clearing away debris and filth from the run-way. One of the officials is out and is talking to the group. It appears he is indicating that some other places need to be repaired."

Luther left the window in the event someone else would like to look out before the sun went down. Sprig tried to see out the window on her tiptoes. She could not reach it. Her comment was one that put Randall high on her list of concerns. "I surly hope and pray that Randall can get in here and not have any trouble landing. Our plane might be the only one we can use within hundreds of miles to get us out of here if need be."

I started to move over to the window to assist Sprig in her desire to look out the window. I was too slow.

Monty moved one of the homemade benches over close to the window. "I will keep a lookout for us until the night closes in. The local men have left the strip and returned to their homes or the local cafe. I feel like I am going to be in big trouble because I don't have a passport. Maybe I can break out of here and go back into the forest."

"Don't try and breakout until we have no other choice." said Sprig as she moved to Monty and put her arms around the lad.

"What if these two G men keep us here even after we show them our passports, said Luther with a twinge of intimidation in his voice?"

Sprig was quick with an answer; "we will cross that bridge when we come to it."

"We would be very prudent if we tried to sleep now so we will be fresh in the morning when Randall comes in. The two benches for two of us and the table for two more is the only arrangement I see to keep us off the floor." I had spotted several mice on the floor in one of the corners but felt it wise not to mention it. The hard surfaces I had indicated would be difficult for sleep without adding the possibility of furry creatures scampering about where no critters should exist. "If you think we need to have someone stand watch I will volunteer to go first."

Luther spoke up first, "I don't think we will need a watch here but if you think it is needed I will go second.

"It's settled then, but we will probably not sleep very sound so if anyone can't sleep just take the third watch, by then it may be morning."

Sprig was doubtful that we could actually meet Randall. "Our passports will have to be shown before they let us out of this room and that would be after Randall had landed. Just so, I am going to try and sleep on the table here to be at my best in the morning. Monty could try to sleep here also. My pack will have to be my pillow. I am so tired I might just get to sleep after all."

The sun had gone down as we talked, leaving the room in near darkness. The locals had all gone home. Earlier, our captors brought in a pot of boiled potatoes and a pitcher of water that consisted of our supper.Luther found a few candles and lighted them to give us some light, helping to burn away the gloom that was trying to settle over us. All was quiet outside with the exception of a ship's horn on the sea down the village's hill.What were we trying to do? Take an old basin back to Jerusalem, stand at the Gate called Beautiful, and just wait for two young men to come up to us and ask us to give them some water. A code for the bundle? It seemed to be too bizarre to work out successfully. We would be in great danger as the Holy Land was not yet settled and peaceful. Even to get into the country without a fuss would be a miracle if we made it. There were times in my life where the events manifested by what surely was a miracle. This time it better be one too.

CHAPTER THIRTY THREE

THE NIGHT PASSED slowly for the four searchers. There was much coughing, tossing, and turning before the morning light began to come through the little window. The sound of a rooster making his presence known by his incessant crowing also came through the window to keep the four from sleeping any longer.

"I suppose it would be too much to ask if we could have fried chicken for breakfast." Luther was not kidding as he looked out the window for any new happenings to report other than his desire for domestic fowl fried to a tender crisp.Little Mr. Monty was next to frame his feelings. "I didn't sleep too well, but I am very hungry for just about anything. My wish is to have something better than boiled potatoes."

"Maybe we need to make enough noise to alert our captors that we are up and ready for some food," Sprig said with a hint of her hunger for food in her eyes. She had eaten very little of the potatoes of last night and now looked at the few that were left with a certain disdain.

Monty was first to implement Sprig's comment into action as he yelled at the top of his voice that they were all hungry. "Hey! Anybody, we up and want to get some food."

No one answered, but they all heard some movement in the next room. The shuffling of shoes came nearer and nearer until a sleepy G-man said to us all, "Shut up or you won't get the breakfast surprise we have for you". With that bit of information, the man was gone to the inner rooms of the building.

"We have a surprise for breakfast. Maybe it will be food this time," said Luther with a twist of hope in his retort.

"I want to see the out side as a free woman as much as I want some food," said Sprig as she looked out the little window.

Waiting for Randall to fly in seemed to take hours but in reality, it was just after a breakfast that the four prisoners wolfed down with relish. Beans and tortillas topped off the breakfast menu straight from some loving chef in the village we later learned. Luther was satisfied with his huge helpings of tortillas and beans. Now he could concentrate on the incoming drone of what must be Randall and the plane. All three of the adults tried to look out the little window to see if the plane was really landing with the Missionary, Randall. The pilot made a visual pass to determine if the strip was worthy of landing. By this time, a small crowd had gathered to witness the event. We knew we could not get out until our passports were shown to the G-men so we could only pray that the landing was successful. The second time around the pilot made a nice three-point landing coming to a stop at the end of the strip. From there, he taxied back to the government building where we all saw Randall shine in all his apparent acclaim as an accomplished airman. This was magnified by the crowd clapping to the addition of four sets of hands emanating from the small window of our cell.

Randall exited the plane and offered to the two G-men his hand of friendship and a sheaf of documents that must certainly contain our passports. The officials looked over the material and smiled as they showed Randal to our quarters. The door opened to a lukewarm apology by the two G-men for the inconvenience we had suffered. Randall followed the two men into the cell. "I hope I am not too late to bring your passports to these two fine gentlemen to affect your release from these confines." The smiles, hugs, and handshakes all around preceded our leaving this holding cell with one little window.

We informed Randall of all of the events leading up to today. He was full of news about the mission and the fact that the miners had been paid and returned to work. A new shipment of meds had also been delivered so that the mission was in fine shape and was being run by her Dad quite efficiently.

"How is daddy? Sprig wanted to know.

"He was very worried about you and wants you to come back to the compound as soon as possible. I told him if you are on a real adventure nothing or no one could get you to quit going forward, like we always do."WE! Where did that WE come from? I was set to ask Sprig about WE and if it meant anything.

"We are having a grand escapade up to now, with all kinds of unusual happenings. I hope to see this through to the conclusion. Just tell dad I am just fine and enjoying myself immensely. I will tell you more about it before you leave for home."I was very pleased to hear Sprig infer that Randal was going back to the mission compound. I had the impression that Randall wanted to tag along on the next leg of our unfinished venture.

Monty was listening to every word trying to see where he fit in the scheme of things. Finally, when the conversations seemed to wane Monty piped up with his strong young voice, "where do I go from here?"

Sprig was the first to go to Monty and allay his uncertainties about what was going to happen next.

"Not to worry my young friend and companion. We will find a way to have you continue with us as we travel by boat up the canal."

Monty gave us all a big smile as Sprig gave him a big hug. She oozed confidence, but I couldn't think how we would accomplish that particular feat.

When Randall had been given all of the details about out venture so far, he was encouraged to fly out while daylight still lingered. Even though Randall was hesitant about leaving, Sprig was insistent that he return to Daddy Gardener and the mission. Sprig continued to talk to Randall while he returned to the plane. Getting in the plane and firing up the engine, he looked rather sad as the little plane taxied down to the far end of the strip. More people came out to watch as well as the two G-men. The little plane shot forward and zoomed overhead in a matter of only a minute or two as he headed south and out of sight.

Now our little group of four headed to a place to camp and formulate the next moves that they must take to get to Jerusalem with their little bundle that had been in Luther's care all this time. Camping out seemed to be more prudent than staying close to the town. As they headed for the wooded area, each participant had the feeling that danger loomed ahead when the next leg of the search was initiated. Only Monty sang a little song of his people that had a happy sound. Was he too naive to know what might lie ahead?

CHAPTER THIRTY FOUR

FINDING A CAMPSITE in the bush was not an easy task. We wanted to have some privacy as well as a secure place to keep any unruly weather elements out of the camp. Finally, Luther and Monty agreed on a small depression that had trees and bushes all around to protect from wind or sand storm that occasionally popped up in this area of the world.

Settling down to camp life, Monty was picking up twigs and branches for a campfire for food and coffee. Luther rewrapped the basin as I took one last look at the map to make certain I had not overlooked any notation or feature on the map. I was tempted to burn it since we had followed it to its apparent conclusion. Sprig looked over my shoulder and gave me what I needed. "You better keep that map for posterity. Some museum will gladly take it for its historical value."

"I don't see anything that we have missed so far and we will keep it for posterity."

She gave me a little hug and said, "good boy."

I wanted to reach up and kiss her for her insightful comments and the power of a little hug. I put that gesture on hold for the time being since the cooking by Luther began to reach my nose. Goat meat from the villagers was in the pan with some beans and dried fruit would give us the food we needed for the next part of our journey.

"One of us will have to go down to the port and get passage to move up to the canal and then on to Israel," said Luther with the completion of frying the meat and beans. Luther was the logical one to go because of his ability to relate to people with his gift of gab and engaging smile.

"We have money to buy passage if they take American dollars. If not we will have to find another way. My suggestion is to stay here at camp and give our extra cash to Luther to buy our way on a ship. He is big and strong to protect our investment so that Sprig and I with Monty too can get on with our search for those two men in Jerusalem."

Luther beamed with pride at my assessment of his attributes and abilities. Sprig nodded her head in agreement as she portioned out food to Monty's awaiting plate. Monty recognized the considerate gesture with, "Thanks, Miss Sprig. When will Mr. Luther begin his getting passage for us?"

Sprig wanted to say, "right a way," but she looked at Luther for some sort of sign but without success.

I caught the glimpse and said, "You could go now if you wanted to. We all have some money from when Randall brought some clothes and supplies." I gave most of my cash to Luther as Sprig followed suit.

"Well it looks like I am elected to trudge down to the docks to see if any ships will land soon on their way up to the canal and over to the Holy Land. I will buy tickets if I can. So wish me God speed and blessings as I take all our money looking for a game of chance at the local dock." Chuckling to himself he turned and began his trek down the hill to the water and the local docks. We all watched with fingers crossed and prayers said under our breath.

"Are there anymore beans." said Monty as he cleaned his plate.

"Sure," said Sprig as she emptied the pan of the beans and meat onto Monty's waiting plate. That boy could eat when he had the chance.

While we waited for Luther we policed the area and tidied up the campsite. Sprig began to write in her journal she had started awhile back. I was curious to see what she had written so far but she always closed the book when I came near.

She gave me that look of innocence and said, "I am just jotting down a few events my dad might be interested in. Some of the plants and trees will give him something to think about when he reads this journal."

That was really my clue to move away so she could write without distractions.

Towards evening Luther came wearily back to camp after walking up the incline from the water. He looked defeated and perturbed.

"My journey has gained very little in the way of progress. Not many ships are due in port for at least a week and the tickets are more of a bribe than an actual price. I think the dock master is in cahoots with the two men in the government house. He said when a ship comes in he signals by three loud blasts from his clarion. We should hear it up here he was certain. I gave little money at this time and propose to wait and see our attitudes for now. We are going to be hanging around a long time with nothing to do, I think."

Sprig said, "We can go back in town and fellowship with the locals. They seemed to like us before. Maybe we can find someone that can grease the skids for us in getting passage on a ship at reasonable prices. They might also know of other ways to get up the coast so we can enter the Holy Land like the nomads do."

"That is a splendid idea," said Luther as his countenance brightened. Even Monty appeared pleased with her idea. I thought her wisdom was very astute as is her physical beauty.

I was also for it and said so. "We have cleaned up here and could go over before dark and strike up some friendships and maybe even find a cozy place to spend the night as it can get cold up here on this ridge."

It was only minutes before we packed up our gear and headed for the town as the sun was going down lazily in the arms of a brilliantly painted sky in the west. A mixture of reds, pinks, and yellows demonstrated the regions tilt towards the desert winds. Even so a most beautiful setting. Coming into town the temperature was ten degrees warmer. The dogs came out to greet us with barking and wagging tails. Men and women came from their homes with shouts of greetings. We certainly were blessed.

One of the couples that had befriended us yesterday was the first to invite us in for some food and drink. All of us agreed at the invitation and soon sat down at a large table where the evening's meal had recently concluded. The plates still were piled full of relishes, flat breads and fruit of all kinds. This was a large family as I remembered. The kids were probably out back playing with some neighbors. As we filled our faces with this generous quantity of food, the hosts poured glasses full of the local fermented juice made from the flowers that only came when the rains poured in the spring.

"This drink is very sweet and tasty," I said as Luther was working on his second glass. "Take it easy Luther we have a long night and day ahead of us," I cautioned Luther while looking at Sprig for confirmation and support.She added her wisdom. "We should not take advantage of our hosts and their hospitality." Looking at Luther with her firm gaze that would melt carbon steel, he lowered his glass. Monty continued to slowly sip his beverage with one eye always on Sprig.The question put to our hosts was very innocent. We asked if any hotels existed in the town for our night's lodging. They insisted we could all stay here for the night. We hesitantly accepted this find with faith and trust our only rationale.

CHAPTER THIRTY FIVE

T HE EVENING WENT smoothly with games, singing, and guitar playing causing many neighbors to attend the festivities. Sprig even danced with a few locals trying to find someone that could steer us to a safe and effective entry into the Holy Land. Luther occupied himself with some food brought in by neighbors. Monty played with several young people his age but he also discreetly made inquiries about ships and nomad routes. He has become a very polished and effective seeker of information. I sat at a table with some older men playing dominoes. Everyone was having such a good time it was a surprise when our hosts called for a ceasing of the activities because of school and work the next day. Most of the folks here worked at a broom factory at the edge of town and thought the employment there was essential to life in this area. Slowly everyone began to return to his or her homes. It was like the leaking of a balloon tire. Slow but steady.

When all the other guests had left the party our hostess wanted to show us our sleeping arrangements. At the first, we tried to refuse but her insistence won out with the promise of a delightful breakfast that sealed the decision to stay. Lunch Box was also very insistent. We were lead to a guest room for two for Luther and I and Sprig got a small room just off the kitchen that had been set up with a cot and other amenities that Magda had made up earlier. Sprig Was Happy with the arrangement. Monty had gone off with a neighbor boy with a promise of school tomorrow. In short, order all was quiet allowing for peaceful sleep until Sprig's scream awakened the entire household. At 2 AM. The scream caused quit a stir. Luther was up and on the run towards the kitchen as was Magda. Sprig was sitting ramrod straight in her bed.

"Someone was trying to gain entrance at the window. When the person left at my scream, he said with a husky voice," 'he would get in later.' Magda was certain it was just a tramp trying to get some food. Sprig took that with a grain of salt as she insisted that one of the boys sit in a chair and provide security before she went back to bed. I was the first to volunteer to Luther's mild disappointment, we all returned to try and sleep the rest of the night. Pulling up the only chair in the small supply room, I made my self-comfortable as Sprig returned to bed and a fitful sleep. I dozed off at about first light to be awakened a short time later by the chastisement of a feminine voice belonging to Sprig. "Wake up oh sleepy guard."I left Sprig's room with her voice of affable scolding, trailing behind me. The entire household gathered in the kitchen for a variable breakfast menu. Pita bread filled with all kinds of good ingredients followed by flatbread and honey. All kinds of fruits and vegetables were also available, grown locally, no doubt. It was difficult to think of our leaving this amicable locale. Monty was still at school so we had to wait awhile until he returned to finalize our future agenda. The window in the supply room was in need of repair and Luther set about with Magda's husband, Chapa. When the repairs were made, Luther and I with Sprig moved away from the house looking for Monty's return, and some views on the days ahead.

"I am certain that when Monty reruns he will have more information about the success of our trip than anything we have gathered as guests of Magda and Chapa," opined Miss Sprig in a very sisterly voice concerning our little friend.

I felt that she was correct in her belief of the young boy who was very talented and adroit.Luther injected the thought about getting into the country and the difficulty of getting a freighter with a pliable captain to allow Monty on board without passport. "I think we will need him on this final journey maybe more than the past weeks," said Luther with much conviction. "He has a grasp of languages and a very gregarious personality that all peoples take to."

Just as we were extolling the virtues of the lad he was spotted bounding down the road with a bevy of boys following him with shouts of laughter."Come over here Monty," I shouted, as the throng attempted to carry him away. With regrets, accompanied by sad faces the group allowed Monty to peel off and come to us. "We need to know if you have any new information that will help us on our way to the Holy Land." He looked excited and ready to burst when all of us looked at him expectantly.

"I know a way. One of my friends gave me this banner. He pulled out a leather banner with scribbling on it. This will give us safe passage with the Bedouins that travel back and forth across the border frontier. Most of the freighter captains will take a bribe to allow us a passage up the sea; here we can jump ship at many points. The whole trip is all set with friends everywhere who will help little Monty."

I could see the boy was getting very confident in his doings. My hope is he does not over play his hand. Both Sprig and Luther were hugging him and congratulating him profusely, adding oil to the fire. "Our first order of business is Luther going down to the docks and find a freighter to sell us passage towards the north. We can only wait a short time in case the two G men up by the airfield have alerted officials of our unorthodox entry into this country. It would be smart to leave the village and camp out on the ridge so the villagers won't be implicated in any way about our clandestine activities in case of official inquires."

Luther surveyed the money situation and then with good wishes from all of us started down towards the docks. Only one old freighter was docked at this time loading up on brooms and coal for ports up in the north, I surmised. The three of us returned to the house to pack up and say our goodbyes. The household was saddened at our departure since we gave only spurious explanations of our departure.

CHAPTER THIRTY SIX

L UTHER WAS GONE most of the day. When he returned on the ridge path we hailed him to come to our new camp. He was not smiling or increasing his gait. When he finally reached us his breathing was rapid and his face crimson. We permitted him to rest a moment before bombarding him with questions.

"Well. What do you have to report?" I fired at him as his demeanor returned to a more normal appearance. He took a deep breath and blurted out that all his money was gone. Someone on the docks asked if he could be of any assistance? When I told him of our need to seek passage on the freighter, he said he would help. When I turned to advance toward the old ship he knocked me down and in my semi confused state he cut and ripped off my money belt. I am so sorry. Later when I came to my senses, I found the captain and told him of my plight. He was not very concerned. He aid it happened quite often. Also, I should be more careful about my recent loss but indicted he would take us on board in the morning if we had more money. I am thinking it will cost us more than half of all we have left.""Don't you worry Luther? We can always get more money if need be. I'm so glad you were not hurt," said Sprig as she felt Luther's forehead

"The main thing is we can leave tomorrow morning to continue our search," I said as kindly as possible, not wanting to diminish Luther's recent ill fortune.

Monty said, "I am ready to go, even if I have no money". His face was bright with anticipation and eagerness. "I can get on that boat without any money or anybody finding me.""No. Monty we will all pay and ride in comparative luxury. I have money that I have kept for just this unexpected occasion. No, need yet to get on or off the ship in a clandestine manner." Since Sprig said it, Monty smiled knowingly even though his vocabulary probably didn't' know what clandestine meant.I knew we would eventually need to exit the ship stealthily when close to the Holy Land. Time enough for that.

We talked as the night approached after a beautiful sunset on our ridge. The night was almost upon us as Sprig set about making supper and boiling coffee. Luther held onto the bundled basin as though someone would try to steal it away at any minute.

"I just dare someone to try and take away this basin before we get to Jerusalem. I feel that it holds some special place in the future of the whole world." Luther was on to some thing that would we find out in end of our search for two young men by the gate called Damascus.

The tent was set up for Sprig while Monty made his usual shelter made of grasses and reeds. Monty insisted Luther and I take his shelter, as he wanted to sleep outside of Sprig's tent for her protection. After a debate, we decided that was a good idea all around. The night passed quietly with no intrusions or problems.

The morning came too quickly as we all dressed and fought to eliminate sleep from our eyes. Luther made a small fire from some twigs that Monty had gathered the day before. It was enough to boil our coffee as we ate left over flatbread and pulled goat jerky. Our plan was to go to the docks early, before any thugs were up to ply their trade. Hot coffee was just strong enough to open the eyes and start the hearts of the weary trekkers. Sprig doled out enough money to Luther for what we supposed the passage would cost us. We had talked about waiting for a better ship but urgency was paramount in our planning. "Let's pack up and be on our way before we change our minds, or if someone from the village should seek us out causing unnecessary delays," I said to hurry the process along. No, need because everyone was packing up like experienced veterans. When all was in readiness, we began our trudge down the ridge to the ancient docks. No one was in sight anywhere although the tired old freighter still hugged to the bleached pier. The way down was longer than I first thought. With some slipping and sliding, we finally came to the decaying wharf and approached the gangplank with some trepidation. Since Luther led the way as Mr. Experience, our fears lessen as he boldly went up the gangplank and shouted for permission to come aboard. A very thin and wiry man came out from the wheelhouse and approached Luther as an old friend. The man was at least of retirement age with a scraggly beard and a balding head. Eyes that might have twinkled in earlier days met our gaze. With little skinny arms outstretched, he attempted to hug Luther, who barely reciprocated the gesture as he held on to his pocket where our money was stashed.

"I see you have returned with your friends to sail with old Raffa and his eloquent sea going vessel, Allabeduin.

I hope you have the money I need to sail through the rough and dangerous sea; Bad weather and patrol boats are constant threats to old Raffa. Sometimes I need monies to supply the patrols for groceries. Come into my office to iron out the details", said the old trader looking more like a huckster every minute.

Just when Luther entered the office, several of the motley crew came up from the hold and gave the rest of us the malevolent eye that reminded me of a dog spying a new delicious bone. Sprig and I stared back with steady looks of Yankee tenacity. The crewmembers finally broke their stare and with apparent indifference slunk back down into the bowels of the freighter just as Luther exited the squat wheelhouse-office.

"We will be on our way in about one hour according to the scheming Captain. He took most of our money. I gave in to one concession. We let him keep our passports and hide if any patrol boats personnel boards the vessel."

"That's two consessions,"I said just to razz Luther. "How can we enter another country without our passports? Said Sprig while keeping Monty from pulling away to explore the ship.

"I think he wants to know when we leave the ship so he can inform any official inquires with the truth to collect a better reward for his information."

"It's just our luck that we get to sail with an enterprising skinflint," said Sprig with a sardonic grin. Within the hour, we set sail to the uneven burping of an ancient steam engine of spurious quality and durability.

CHAPTER THIRTY SEVEN

T HE CAPTAIN FLIPPANTLY had the first officer escort us to our staterooms that looked more like supply closets. Our room had bunk beds and a hammock swinging over some oil drums. Monty claimed the hammock as I took the upper bunk and Luther crashed on the lower bunk to test the rope-spring and straw mattress. "Pretty basic and Spartan but still more comfortable than sleeping on the ground," said Luther with a smirk on his face. "I hope Miss Sprig has a better stateroom. Maybe one with a view."

I looked around our little room and was surprised at the variety of supplies stored in the area, mops, brooms, canvas, chemicals, rope, and other unidentifiable objects. An old fan was on a dilapidated shelf along with maps and charts. "A very important room," said Luther.

Miss Sprig came by and invited us to see her room. "I have a better room than this," she said with little or subtly arrogance. Sprig led us out of the storage-locker-Room, onto an upper deck that was quiet and not smelly. Her cabin had been one of the officers, so that the amenities though meager where evident. A bed instead of a bunk was the first bit of comfort seen. A small desk close to a clothes locker made the area comfy. In the corner was a small but functioning lavatory with cold and hot water sans bath or shower, probably down the passageway. Sprig was delighted with her new room complete with a porthole and working ceiling fan. Monty, Luther, and I looked around and felt cheated and uneasy. Was this comparative splendor a precursor to possible advances of the captain or his first mate towards Sprig? None of us said anything, knowing Sprig would just brush it off as nothing to worry about. "I can take care of myself," would be her predicable answer. After the tour, we all decided to scout out the galley and dining area just to satisfy our curiosity since our stomachs began to make gastric sounds of need. On the main deck, we finally located what appeared to be a saloon with a small galley next to it. A Chinese cook was busy with chores in the galley that we surmised was lunch. The smells were strange but pleasant to us. "I don't suppose he needs any help," said Sprig.

"I think he would rather we not interrupt his routine or any crew member, was the informed comment of Luther." The captain said that none of us should hinder any of his crew in anyway. Our best course would be to observe the routine of the ship before we do anything on our own. I still have my backpack on. Do you think there is any safe pace to store our little object of interest?" I gave my suggestion. "A place that the captain would show us would be privy to the first mate and captain, both would pursue their curiosity and begin to ask a lot of questions upon discovery of a possible art object. The safest place would be out in the open. Sprig, could you put it in your room out in the open with a plant or some similar unobtrusive object in it to disguise its real value?

"I could place it on my little desk and put all kinds of things in it. Paper, pencils, hair stuff, and any other small items that will hide the real object's use."

While we had been touring the ship, the Captain had slipped his moorings and we were headed out to sea. The old engine huffed and puffed as the coal-fired steam turbines came to life. All of us decided to find a deck chair to wait out lunchtime. When we found a few chairs on one of the upper decks, they looked like they had come from some trash heap. They still worked even though the location was such as to render the smoke with its grit and grime a constant menace to deal with. Luther kept a close watch on the door to the dinning area in case the crew failed to notify us of the time of serving of food. After about 20 minutes, the two ship's officers went to the saloon and appeared to receive food from the Chinaman. We looked at other and nodded towards the dinning room and as one unit we simultaneously got up and headed for lunch. The men in the room looked at us as though we were intruding into their inner sanctum. The Captain eventually got up and waved his hand around the room, including the Chinaman, with the effect all of this was ours. We nodded in appreciation. We found a table and had the Chinaman bring us the lunch or was it grub? Luther was the first to comment. "Oh Look! Fried rice and beans with bits of fish. A scrumptious lunch if ever I had one."

Monty was digging in and making sounds of contentment. "Just like my old auntie use to make."

Regardless of our own personal appraisal of the food, we ate ample portions with little knowledge this would be our daily sustenance. Afterwards, we all returned to our assigned lodgings to assess what lay ahead. Monty felt excluded, so he naturally began to make forays around the ship for a kind of reconnaissance. Sprig took the bundle from Luther and proceeded to set it on her desk with all kinds of knick-knacks and odds and ends to make it appear innocuous. The two of us in the supply room-state room took down some of the maps and charts to refresh ourselves on the unfamiliar territory we would be entering. Luther made a lot of notes as we pointed out places of interest. Monty had obtained some writings at the village that would give us safe passage with the Bedouins. We had to find a jumping off place and a way through the wastelands of the Judean Wilderness. After making copious notes, we replaced the maps and charts on the shelf, making them appear undisturbed. Luther and I made plans to secrete food and water for the trip. It was difficult to find ways to store food and water, even with Sprig and Monty's help. Jars and bottles became very arduous to locate and put in deep pockets so no one would be the wiser. After four or five days, we had accumulated enough to seriously decide on a day and hour to vacate the old freighter. Monty was to retrieve our passports if able from the Captains cabin and cabinet safe. He accomplished his task with great skill. At 3 AM on the tenth day, at sea, we planned to jump over board as we had noticed a few shore lights. "Lets take one of the row boats instead of swimmimg,"said Luther looking down at the coal black water and the distant lights.

We very carefully released an old rowboat and silently lowered it into the water on a side not viewed by the wheelhouse. Going down a rope ladder into the little rowboat it was only minutes later the freighter was chugging out of our line of sight. As we rowed towards shore, our only concern was if the Captain reported us for lifting our passports and stealing a rowboat. These concerns quickly became insignificant as a patrol boat along the shore played a searchlight on the water ahead of us.

CHAPTER THIRTY EIGHT

THE PATROL BOAT was fast and moved up the coast with its swinging searchlight scanning the beach and adjacent water. "When the boat is far down the coast let's row like crazy to reach the shore before they return their patrol," was the best advice I could offer as we began to paddle with a certain frenzy even before my redundant recommendation. With this kind of energy focused on rowing, we gained the beach in a very short time. We pulled the little boat far up the beach as the patrol boat came back with its roving eye. The light passed over us but since our boat and we huddled down behind some scrub bushes the boat continued on its way.

Monty was the first one on up the beach sand dune, encouraging us to hurry up to get inland. "Come on my friends. My map tells me to go this way. We are far down the coast. We jumped off too soon so we will have to walk a lot before sun comes up." "I didn't want hear that," said Sprig as we all trudged through the soft sand making headway difficult. The land soon turned hard under our feet as Monty led us inland and north according to Luther's compass. The lad was adept at reading his map so we let him lead us on into the night with only starlight for illumination. His young eyes were a blessing to all of us. We came to an area near the Dead Sea when daylight found us hot and tired. We found a wadi and bedded down for the heat of the day to pass.

The wilderness has its own torment as we determined our water supply to be inadequate to take us very far in this heat. We would head for En Gedi as fast as possible when night fell knowing a spring was there, according to Monty's map. The evening found us just as tired and unprepared as when we crawled into the wadi this morning. Picking up ourselves, we stumbled out of the wadi only to find a band of local Bedouins moving towards the Dead Sea with all of their possessions. When they spotted us, all was deathly still as their march stopped as though they were frozen in time.

We also stopped in our tracks waiting to see who would make the first move. To our astonishment, Monty began to run towards the band of travelers shouting and waving his map and paper in the air. The lad showed no fear or aversion to the fierce looking group with staffs, pikes, and other weapons being waved in the air shouting threats. We all were spellbound as Monty reached the group without any harm to his body. They did gather him up and carry him out of our sight. "Do you suppose they will harm our young friend?" Said Sprig with more emotion than her face reveled. "I don't think we could over power the band but maybe we should at least approach them with a white flag of truce."

Luther was also concerned when he said, "let's go up and make friends with them. Maybe they have some extra food to share with us."

I felt that we should wait a little while and then approach them with the white flag as Sprig had suggested. "Sprig, can you find a white item to be our flag of truce?"

"Sure, but it may have to be one of my undies. Do you think that will offend them?"

"No. They probably don't know what undies are. I will buy you some more for your trousseau before we get married." Sprig looked at me with a fading doubt in her eyes as the thought began to take shape in her mind.

Therefore, with a pair of undies tied to a stick we advanced toward the gathered band of Bedouins. They didn't move or frown or smile or anything. Our presence did affect them because woman and children had gathered behind the tall leaders. When we reached the group, they parted to channel us back to a place where Monty stood with a massive man that oozed leadership. He was tall with a beard, wide forehead, generous smile that showed a perfect set of white teeth. At the end of the channel, Monty was smiling. Women and children surrounded him. Monty radiated the epitome of confidence and triumph. Holding up his papers he shouted to us above the clamor and excited Bedouins, "they want to help and accompany us to the area of the Great City. They recognized my map and the paper that I got back in the village. The writer of my paper was a relative of this great man before us. Abdullah is his name. The young man next to him knows English and will translate for you. Armenia is his name." "We have much to talk about," I said as the great man motioned us to enter his tent for formalities and welcome. In the tent made of goatskins we talked for quite a while, explaining most of our mission. Hot sweet tea was served with little honey cakes that gave Luther big smiles and copious thanks to our host. Sprig optioned to stay outside with the great mans wives, not wanting to offend the male dominated society. It was decided that we stay with the band for several days before advancing towards civilization. Abdullah was not very keen on getting too close to the authorities of the land. "Too much war," he had said.

So, for the next three days we rested and enjoyed the hospitality of the tribe. Two men from the tribe ventured out to see how the authorities responded to the political situation of the day. On their return, they said that checkpoints still remained and were manned by soldiers. On each hill was a jeep with at least two men in attendance, It will be impossible to enter the city undetected was their conclusion. "I wondered if we could get in under darkness."

"No. They are just as diligent if not more so, after dark when surrounding enemies try to infiltrate the borders."

"I guess our only hope is prayer and perfect concealment."

With this in mind, Abdulla suggested a monastery in one of the Wadi's nearer the city.

"Those brothers have free range around the area. They could get you in better than any other means, I am sure,"

So, we prepared to travel to the wadi where the monastery was situated. The young man that knew English said he would go with us to introduce us to the brothers and explain our quest.

In the morning, we set out for our long hot trek. Leaving Monty behind at his request as well as ours, we followed our leader. Armenia set a fast pace, knowing the heat would slow us down later in the day. Keeping us low in wadis and boulders, we evidently passed by any scrutinizing eyes. Towards evening, we had passed the Dead Sea and skirted Jericho going to the entrance to the Wadi. With out tongues hanging out we begged to rest before going on. Armenia wanted us to continue before any hilltop military spotted us. "If you must rest, I will go ahead and announce our presence to the brothers so you can approach safely later on. When you approach the buildings, you will be met by a couple of Guinea Fowl that will sound the alarm for the monastery. The sound is loud and startling. Not to fear, they will bring the brothers to you." With those words of caution and secreting us in a cleft behind some boulders, the young man moved up the wadi to a set of buildings precariously hugging the canyon wall in the distance. We felt alone in this rugged land with no one to vouch for us or encourage us. We really missed Monty's enthusiasm.

CHAPTER THIRTY NINE

W E RESTED FOR about an hour. The day had taken something out of Luther and I. Even Sprig was all tuckered out jumping over rocks and sweating to deplete her hydration reserves. Eventually, to Sprig's encouragement we began our trek up the narrow canyon or wadi, after resting a few hours. The day was still hot but breezes began to move up the wadi. A considerable time later, we found ourselves serenaded by two Guinea Fowl with piercing sounds of alarm. It was evening with the sky ablaze with copper fire. Two brothers appeared out of nowhere to bow and motion for us to follow them. Armenia was nowhere to be seen as we gained what appeared to be a gate and the entrance to the building precariously hanging on the canyon wall. Moving through the gate, we were amazed at the complexity of the structures that greeted us. With steps and ramps, we were led to a cluster of small rooms that would be our home for several days. Our guide motioned each one to take a room. The rooms were more like cells and they must be for visitors or monks that wanted solitude and privacy for they were sparse at best. One narrow bed with an overhead shelf for icons and books gave the room some character. The room was complete with a small milking stool for reading or meditating. Unpacking took no time, as I was curious to see Luther and Sprig's accommodations. Peering into the other cubicles I was saying with a smile on my face, "I see we all got the luxury suites as is our custom." Luther replied with the same silly smile on his face. "I think the bed may be too short. I'll have to curl up like a snail to get my much needed rest."Sprig was happy with her room. "I won't have to listen to your loud snoring when I close my door."I hoped she meant Luther and not me. She had not looked at anyone in particular so that was a relief for my amorous advances.

"Let's find a meeting room or a place where some bodies might be breathing. I am ready for some food and information on how we are to gain the city above." Lunch Box was living up to his name. The three of us moved down the stone passageway until we came to a balcony. Looking over the railing, we spied Armenia in an expressive discussion with a very tall and important looking brother who must be the leader or superior of the monastery. When Armenia saw us, he waved us down to the large room below. When we had gathered together with the two we were introduced to Brother Barnabas, the Rector of this community. "He has told me that the only way you can gain entrance to Jerusalem is by hiding in a cart of hay and vegetables that goes up and back about every seven days. His recommendation is that only one person try to hide as the vendor will have to be paid per person, a substantial sum."

"Will he take dollars?" Was my question "I hope Sprig, that you still hold an ample amount of money for this last leg of our search"?

Brother Barnabas spoke to Armenia who told us that the vendor would willing to take dollars as he is a very wily and crafty man of many talents.

Sprig gave her nod that she had a sufficient amount of money still in her possession. The only thing left now was to wait for the vendor and decide who would go up to the city with our prize. We followed the two men to another room that was the dinning room. Plates of food and bread graced the table where we were ushered. Great mugs of pomegranate juice sat before each plate for our liquid refreshment. A real treat after so much hot sweet tea we had over the last few days in the desert. Afterwards we were shown to a library where we were expected to read until bedtime. Luther was very fortunate to find a volume with pictures. Sprig and I had to be content with Greek texts, which were slightly familiar. No radio, no games, not even a puzzle to put together. A short time later, a bell was heard signifying bedtime so we retired.In the morning, we began the routine of eating, sleeping, walking around the grounds waiting for the wily vendor to show up. The three of us met several times to appoint one to go with the crafty vendor. The third meeting found me as the designate to go with our relic to the gate and wait for two young men to ask if I had a gift for them.The waiting lasted three days, a time that we used to try and figure out how to get out of the country, and back to Sprig's dad's mission. A dilemma with no uncomplicated answer. We would have to pray again for some more miracles.On the third day, an old man with a cart and donkey disturbed the Guiana Fowl to a shrill and effective alarm. He had a cart that was being loaded with vegetables; that the brothers had raised on little terraces cut into the canyon. He brought hay for the goats from which the brothers made cheese to sell in the city along with the vegetables. The hay would stay here except a small amount to hide a passenger from prying eyes. Barnabas and the old vendor talked for a long time to arrange my entry into the city.

Sprig was called on to give the old man a large sum of money for the task ahead. The old man's name was Isaac and he giggled a lot as the money changed hands and directed me to the cart to get under the hay. He had to unhitch the cart from the donkey to be able to turn around in such a limited space. The hay seemed to be not much cover I thought. When I began to slip, under the hay Isaac motioned for me find a board on the floor, pull it up, and get into the cavity beneath. Doing as indicated by hand gestures, I found a box on the underside of the cart. If ever a box looked like a casket this one did. I squeezed into the casket-box as I heard my friends wish me luck. The basin as wrapped in rags per Barnabas's suggestion and it lay by my head in a tight fit. Breathing in the smell of old hay, the cart moved up the wadi. I was jostled and jolted so much I almost lost my breakfast, my body thinking it was on a rolling jerking ship. We passed several checkpoints with no trouble, as the sentries appeared to be interested in other matters. The result of prayer?

CHAPTER FORTY

OLD ISAAC MOVED the cart through narrow streets until we came to a place that was finally quiet. Here he talked to a man and unloaded the vegetables. After a short time he came back to the cart and said, "out Joe, out." I lifted the boards and got up and out of the cart into a dark street with no one around. Isaac led me to a little lean-to hovel that was his abode. Inside was a bed and table. He threw some blankets on the floor and indicated it was my bed. As I lay down, he brought to me a crust of bread and some goat cheese. This was my supper. It was going to be some long days before my odyssey was completed. I decided to get some sleep and get up early in the morning to begin my wait at the Damascus gate.

The morning came quickly. I found some more bread and cheese and a jug of water by my bedroll. Old Isaac was up and puttering around out side with his cart. When I approached him, he gave me a robe, a turban, and a crutch. He helped me dress appropriately and then motioned to follow. I had to go back and fetch my wrapped relic before going off after the old man. Dressed like so many others in rags we passed through the throng of people on the way to the gate where I was to sit collecting alms and waiting for two young men to ask me if I had a gift for them. By the time we got to the gate, I was using a crude crutch and stooping over to the giggles of the old vendor. I sat down and began my vigil near he gate. Isaac left me to my own thoughts and deeds. I spent the day here gathering a few coins and a backache. With no success at evening time, I was glad to see Isaac come and jerk his head to follow him. Getting up and limping with my head down I followed the heels of the old man back to the shed he called home. My back was hurting as I sat on his sleeping cot and ate bread, cheese and bits of fish that might have at one time been living in a sewer, The two of us tried to have a conversation without much luck. The exercise did make nighttime and bedtime come quickly. The following day was a duplicate of the previous one. Still no success. I was beginning to doubt my activity. On the third day in the morning, a soldier came to me and asked me something that I did not understand. He poked at my leg with a frown on his face, The man next to me who I had not talked to at anytime, gave the soldier some gestures that signified I was deaf and dumb as well as crippled. This satisfied the soldier who then left my neighbor and me. My neighbor smiled as he showed me he had no legs that had been covered. Leprosy of the worst kind I thought. About noontime when it was very hot and many were eating a midday meal, two young men approached my neighbor and gave him some coins. They turned to me as the neighbor was scrabbling for the coins and very quietly asked if I had a present for them. I was surprised but more than ready to give up the relic to those two. They received it, rags, and all and then disappeared in the noonday crowd. I wanted to leave right away but thought it best to wait for Isaac. My back was very painful but I was reminded by my neighbor to be thankful for the things I had. This made my back feel better. The old vendor came punctually at evening time and led me back to the shed. He giggled and smiled when he noticed the rag-wrapped parcel gone. With a wave of his hands, he gave out a grunt of satisfaction and pointed down towards the monastery. I assumed my stay at the Hotel Limited was about to cease. I dreaded the ride down in the casket but being reunited with my friends would certainly compensate my discomfitures.

In the morning, the cart was ready with its hiding place and several new bundles of hay. Crawling under the hay and into the waiting sarcophagus I got as comfortable as possible, considering the old cart was evidently made from scrap pieces of wood. I was pleased that the absence of the relic gave me a little more headroom. Just as I thought we were to begin our trip down the wadi a voice that sounded very military called for Isaac to stop. When stopped, I caught some words that asked the old vendor to bring back some extra vegetables for the soldier and his group. Isaac was very cordial leaving the area with a hearty *Shalom* for the soldier.My brain was constantly trying to figure out a way to leave the country and return home or at least to Sprig's father's mission.

CHAPTER FORTY ONE

THE RIDE IN the old rickety cart was very bumpy over the cobbled streets of the city, complete with occasional bone jarring steps. The cart itself was wobbly, waiting for its final days not too far in the future to just fall apart in the ancient dust in this ancient land. With little effort, I could see through the slats to the road or trail beneath the ancient transport. We finally came to the wadi and its well-worn way that gave me some relief. The heat of the day began to seep in my enclosure with a vengeance to all that rode this way surreptitiously. The Guinea Fowl hens gave out their terrible shrieking for a warning to the brothers in the monastery as we approached the cluster of gray buildings. The sounds outside soon gave me the voices of my friends as well as the head—Brother of the community. Old Isaac attended to business while I cooked in the cart's casket. He began unloading his hay and taking orders for the vegetables for his return trip. I almost thought he had forgotten me when Sprig appeared after taking off the hay.

Looking at me with a smile that would melt hardened steel she gave me a cooling question. "What have you been doing?" Her voice was like music and even more melodic than I had remembered. "We thought you might have stayed longer in your sumptuous lodgings while we suffered inconveniences here." Sprig had a sense of humor that I would like in my future wife. She helped me out of the casket with a gentleness that spoke volumes to me. Lunch Box was on hand with a pomegranate in hand that was dripping juice onto his chin as it was devoured. With outstretched arms, he gave me a bear hug and spoke in my ear.

"Did all go well as we were instructed by the three amigos to give up the basin to two young men?"

"Yes. It went off like clockwork. Now all we have to do is find a way home or to Sprig's dad without landing in a prison." Armenia attended the gathering and told us that the Bedouins had moved to another position. "You should try and find them as soon as possible before they move too far away."

Knowing Monty was with them gave me a feeling of desperation.

Dickson Straight was not known to be desperate about anything but Monty has been the real force behind our advance and success. To leave without the little guy would be a travesty that would haunt me for years to come. I knew Sprig and Luther felt the same. "Let's clean up and pack up to begin our search for Monty and away out of this ancient land." The comment fell on concurring ears as my two friends murmured agreement. With much rushing, about to get food and water we packed and hastily thanked our benefactors and then moved out with our guide, Armenia. The day was hot with no rain insight. A few birds soared overhead looking for a meal or shade, I thought. The Jordan valley lay before us in ancient reckonings. Armenia made a sweeping arc with his hands and said, "no one in sight."

We had to skirt Jericho if we were not to be seen, Armenia made the correct adjustments and muttered that, and "the Bedouins would have to find us"

Traveling behind heaps of sand and dirt, we left Jericho undetected. Armenia spotted the Bedouin tents in the far distance and gave out a muffled cry of victory. The tents were positioned in a wadi on the banks of the great salt sea. The thinnest of trails of smoke lifted lazily in the hot, stifling atmosphere telling us hot tea awaited our arrival and reunion with Monty. Approaching the tents, we were met by one very happy boy. Monty gave hugs all around to show his appreciation of our return. Only Sprig and Monty exhibited a tearful reunion that was very emotional.

Entering the leader's tent where tea was passed around to all, including Sprig. Old Abdulla welcomed us and his friend Armenia using many words and gestures. After all of the amenities the old man told us about a new town on the red sea where we might find some transportation to another land. Through Armenia translating, the old leader inferred he could take us near the new town and show us the way after leaving the Family of Bedouins. Armenia added that many resort divers from all over come there to dive. Maybe we could secure a ride out from one of the charter groups. With this shaky plan in place, we talked of other things culminating in siestas for everyone. The evening brought some more goat meat and cheese with goats milk as a chaser. When night came, it was conducive to just go lay down for no real lights stabbed the beautiful desert night sky. Each of us lay on our backs and watched the stars play their brilliant ballet more splendid than any city sky.

In the morning, we packed up after an early breakfast and headed south for EILAT on the red sea. The Bedouins left us several miles from the town. Many thanks were given. Monty being especially was saddened by the departure for he had made many friends while in their keeping. The trek towards the touristy town was hot and arduous. We made the outskirts in the afternoon where we hid behind some huge mounds. Luther, chosen to go in a try to find us a way to leave the country surreptitiously left when the night began to fall to cover his advance upon unsuspecting resort revelers. Later that night Luther returned with grins that indicated success. "I have found an American millionaire who has a chartered aircraft. He indicted if we can get by the Airstrip sentries, the plane would be open for us to enter and hide. He will plot a flight plan to Madagascar and then veer off to land at the mission, drop us off, and continue on to his flight plan destination."

"How many sentries did you see for us to get past?" My question was one that we all wanted to know.

"I only saw two but there may be more."

Sprig was the one to add, "We only need to be careful and pray a lot."

"We will have to go tonight because he is to fly out tomorrow with or without us. When I told him that four of us would need to be hidden, he laughed and said the diving gear was in the back of the plane and afforded many nooks and crannies to hide in."

We waited until the wee hours of the morning giving us what little advantage we had. Moving stealthily out and down towards the airfield the sentries seemed to be busy looking at the stars and did not notice our advance and entry into the twin-engine plane. Finding the jumbled diving gear, we each found a concealed area and rested or slept. When the planes engines started, one sentry came on board and gave a cursory sweep for regulations sake. Soon the big bird was going down the runway and we were on our way home.

Chapter Forty Two

S PRIG LAID HER head on my shoulder as we winged our way back to the mission. I spoke sweet nothings in her ear as she slept. When the plane landed, Randall and father both came out with quizzical countenances. We left the plane with many thanks and offers of money to our benefactor, which he gracefully refused.I needed to ask Mr. Gardener for Sprig's hand in marriage before I took my courting to the next level. After all the welcoming celebrations, I asked Mr. Gardener if I could speak to him in private. When Alone I put the question to him.

"Sir, I would like your permission to court Sprig and marry her with you blessings."

The elder man laughed at me and then apologized. "You should know by now that that young lady has a mind of her own and my blessings would be a small consent to the permission to woo my daughter. But go ahead and do your best. I would like some grandchildren before I die. By the way Randall is an ordained minister if you think you will need one before you leave."

The meeting went off better than expected. Rejoining my group, Luther looked at me with questioning eyes.

Sprig looked at me and smiled. Monty was getting ready to return to the jungle. The lad was tearful as we all gave him hugs and kisses. "Monty you have been one exceptional boy. If you get to the States in the future please look us up for a reunion, said Sprig while wiping a tear or two. Without another word, the lad moved off into the jungle and disappeared before our very eyes.

I took Sprigs hand asking her to walk with me around the compound. The air was warm and breezy with some jungle fragrances wafting across the compound. A beautiful bird winged his way over our heads as he made pleasant sounds. "Sprig I want to marry you if you will have me. We will have an exciting life and a bunch of kids. I can't offer money or riches but I will cherish you always and protect, provide, and pamper you for all the years we are together."

Sprig was quick to reply, "how many in a bunch? Well you finally got it out. I think I will be your wife but let's wait awhile to be sure. We have been through a lot that might alter our reasoning. We can have a church wedding in the States.

And we did. Mr. Gardener gave Sprig a way. Luther was best man. He eventually became a world-class chef, while Monty we heard was preparing to be a translator for the UN. Sprig and I became fulltime missionaries with three children of our own. Not quite a bunch but enough. We waited for any news about the two young men in Jerusalem and the foot-washing basin. We might have to wait until prophecy is fulfilled as in Revelations 11:3

The End